DARK WISH

CLARISSA WILD

PLAYLIST

"Something In The Way (Epic Trailer Version)" by
Samuel Kim Music

"Suspicious Minds" by KI: THEORY

"Burning Down The House" by KI: THEORY

"Pressure" by MISSIO

"Nature" by MISSIO

"The Plan" by Travis Scott

"Jit Thin" by Ruby My Dear

"Dinner & Diatribes" by Hozier

"In The Woods Somewhere" by Hozier

"Dangerous Game" by Klergy

"L'Aérogramme de Los Angeles" by Woodkid & Louis
Garrel

"Lost In The Fire" by Gesaffelstein & The Weeknd

"Too Late" by The Weeknd

"Light Of The Seven" by Ramin Djawadi

"Main Theme – Westworld" by Ramin Djawadi

"The Dog Is Black" by UNKLE (Dial:Molotov Remix)

PROLOGUE

ELI

"Stop."

A moment in time never stops, yet I still request it to.

My driver parks the car along the side of the road while I peer out the window.

As I wait, I finally see what I spotted when I told him to stop.

The girl who made me do a double take.

From her dark hair that loosely falls over her shoulders to her apple cheeks and red-painted lips that make her look like a porcelain doll, she stands out from the sea of people walking in the opposite direction.

With a simple glance, she's taken my breath away, and I want to know her name.

It's not often that I want to step out of my world and into hers, that I want to know what she sounds like when she's touched, that I want to brush away those gentle locks and whisper promises in her ear that I cannot keep.

That a predator has found its prey.

My Adam's apple bobs in my throat as though the excitement has risen to my throat. It isn't a surprise, but I must contain myself.

Too precious … too innocent …

But not forever.

No girl is perfect, not even when they look like her.

No, I will catch her in a lie, in dishonor, in jealousy, in dirt.

I will catch her when she falls, and when she does, I will pick her up and bring her into my world.

***

Amelia

I never thought I'd beg a stranger to give me pain.

Give me pleasure.

Give me all and more.

Take from me what you desire.

Take from me until I am an empty, soulless vessel.

Because that is what I deserve, what I yearn for with every fiber of my being.

As I sit here on his lap with my hands tied, my body straining against his while he slides a knife across my skin, I whimper.

"Please … punish me," I plead with this man.

This man who took me away from my home into the dark of night.

This man who treats me like a pet, like he owns me.

This man … who knows my worst secret.

A secret buried deep inside.

My deepest, darkest sin.

And the man who's come to claim my punishment.

ONE

Amelia

When you see the one you know is going to turn your world upside down, you know.

I always thought people were joking when they said that.

But I know now that I was wrong. So wrong.

Because as I place some returned books back on the shelf where they belong, I notice a guy sitting at one of the round tables in the far back, where usually no one comes. I stick my head out and peek at him while he's reading a book, casually slanted in his chair. One firm hand clutches the book while the other touches his stubbly chin. His tongue dips out and wets his thin lips, and he rubs them together while staring at the pages. My eyes immediately home in on the title of the book. An obvious bodice ripper, it's a book I wouldn't expect a man like him to read.

Because what a man he is, all suited up, looking expensive as heck, with his golden watch and perfect black shoes. His slick brown hair combed back with gel makes him look almost like a rich and powerful politician reading a very spicy romance novel. What are the odds?

Suddenly, his green eyes peer up from the pages and bore straight into mine.

My eyes widen, and panic floods my veins.

I immediately step back, hiding behind the bookcase again, and I close my eyes while my heart races in my chest.

I wasn't watching. I swear I wasn't looking at this gorgeous man. And he didn't see me.

Right?

But when I open my eyes again, there he is, right in front of me.

"Can I help you?" His voice is low—like dark chocolate you want to lick off someone's body low—and it makes me gulp.

Staring at him for a moment, I slowly part my lips, but words fail to come to my mind. The stranger is so handsome up close that he takes my breath away.

I shake my head.

He leans in, tilting his head. The intoxicating scent of expensive cologne reminiscent of luscious trees and green forests fills my nostrils, almost pulling me in closer for another whiff.

"Are you sure?"

I shudder, my body inching back from the sheer power he exudes. His mere proximity is making me sweat, and my eyes can't stop looking at all the tiny details, like the excited glimmer in his eyes and the hint of a smirk on his lips.

I nod a few times. "Sorry, I didn't mean to—"

"Stare?" he interjects.

I swallow hard in response.

A brief smile appears on his face. He holds out the book he was just reading. I gaze at it for a moment, wondering what he wants from me.

"You're a librarian, aren't you?" he says. "Would you put this back for me, please?"

My cheeks turn crimson red again. "I, uh … of course." When I take the book from him, our fingers briefly touch, and it feels as though lightning just shot up into my veins.

"Thank you," he says, and the smile that follows reminds me of a wolf showing its canines. "I can appreciate someone who does their job thoroughly."

I swallow hard.

I didn't want to, but my body responds so strongly to everything he says and does that it feels as though I'm forced. Like a magnet relentlessly pulled closer to him.

Suddenly, he leans in and whispers into my ear, "I will see you soon."

My heart drops into my shoes as the stranger walks off and leaves me breathless.

Who was that man? And what did he mean by *see you soon*?

***

Eli

It wasn't an accident that I was there at that exact moment in time.

She may think it was, but she concocted that lie in her head to make the idea I was there in the first place palpable.

There was only one reason for me to be present in that library, and it wasn't to read some book. Sure, I picked a random one up just for the fun of it, but reading wasn't my goal.

It was a means to an end.

That book allowed me to blend in and wait … until she finally laid her eyes on me.

I just wanted to see how she'd react. What kind of look she'd throw my way once she saw that I was there not just to read but also to engage with her.

I couldn't stop myself, even if I wanted to. I was that turned on by the mere look in her eyes and the way her body yielded to mine as though it was always meant for me and me alone. As if it knew it belonged to me.

But I must wait.

Hold off.

Be patient.

It's not my best asset, but it's what must be done.

Because I have to know what kind of person she truly is. The real sinner beneath that perfect angelic veneer.

***

Amelia

After my shift finishes at the library, I run home for a quick microwave meal before my nighttime job at Joe's Hotties. A girl's gotta do what a girl's gotta do to survive.

Besides, it pays the bills. And the very hefty college student loans I still have to pay off.

My grandparents didn't leave me an inheritance. They gave all the money to a company and never told me why.

So I have no choice but to work as hard as I can and be proud of myself.

When I get there, I put on my apron and wait for the orders to come in. My phone suddenly vibrates in my pocket, and I take it out and check who it is.

Chris?

I haven't heard from him in hours. He's always so busy with work. In fact, I don't think we've said more than a few words to each other in days. He's always on the run and never home. Why would he suddenly call?

"Hey," I say as I pick up.

"Hi, just wanted to tell you I won't be home on time tonight, so go to bed without me. 'Kay?"

Nothing new there. "Okay. Anything else?"

"No, I'm in an important meeting, so don't call me."

He hangs up the phone before I can respond, and I don't know why but that still surprises me.

It shouldn't bother me. I knew I didn't come first when I started dating him, but somehow, someway, I believed he would change over time.

Sometimes, I really wish he wouldn't call me while I was at work. But it's really his shtick not to care about my times. Just like he doesn't care about virtually anything I do … or say … or want. Sometimes, I wonder why we're together at all. Or if he even likes me beyond the sex—which isn't even that great, if you ask me. In and out, wham bam, thank you, ma'am. That's it.

And he always gets so angry with me for no apparent reason—mismatched socks, burned food, missing keys—all of which he takes out on me. But then he comes home with these gifts again and again and reminds me that he loves me, so I forgive him.

"Amelia," the bartender calls, pulling me from my thoughts, "table sixteen. In the back."

"Got it," I reply. Picking up the glass and bowl of nuts, I move between all the customers eagerly watching the show on stage. Some of them slap my bum when I walk past, but it doesn't even faze me anymore. When I first started out here, it took me a long time to feel comfortable in my own skin wearing these skimpy clothes and having all these men stare at my boobs and touch my ass, but I've grown used to it.

At least here I get touched. At home, not so much.

I walk up to my first customer of the day, smile happily, and say, "Here you go, sir." I place the drink and bowl of nuts in front of him.

"Oh … the other girl gone or something?" he asks, grabbing a handful of nuts and shoving them in his mouth, chewing loudly.

"I'm taking over her shift," I reply, clearing my throat. "But don't worry, I'm more than happy to serve you."

He looks me up and down and licks his lips, then swallows. "Yeah … you'll do …"

Suddenly, he grabs my waist and pulls me closer, forcing me down on his lap.

"Sir, please," I say, still trying to stay polite even though he's manhandling me. "Don't."

"What's your problem? This's what you're here for, right?" He fiddles with my top to try to get the buttons to pop, but I move away out of his arms. However, he forces me right back down onto his lap again, his grip too strong for me.

"C'mon, just a peek."

"Sir, please, stop. I am just a waitress," I say, turning around to look at him so I can reason with him. "There are plenty of girls on and off stage who—"

"Fuck those girls, I want a private dancer," he murmurs

in my ear, clearly already intoxicated. "C'mon, do a little lap dance for me, will you?"

Sometimes I give them to customers, yes, but not guys who are so drunk and rowdy they can't keep their hands off. I don't want to fight him, but if I have no choice … should I do it? Knowing I could lose my job?

"Let her go."

His booming voice is the first thing I hear before I actually see him. The man who was seated in the adjacent booth is now leaning against this booth. A buff man in a suit with slick brown hair, a strong, square jaw, and smoldering green eyes. A man who instantly takes my breath away … because it's *him*. The guy I saw at the library.

I've seen plenty of guys come and go in this club, but none quite as expensive-looking as him, and he seems totally out of place.

I freeze even though I'm still seated on the lap of a drunken stranger.

Something about this man feels dangerous … almost exciting.

"What the fuck do you want?" the guy holding my waist says to the man.

The man's thin lips twitch, almost as if he intended to smirk but then stopped himself right before he did. His eyes narrow, and he reaches into his pocket. Slowly, he takes out a gun with a silencer on it and points it right at the stranger.

My eyes widen, and I gasp in shock.

He puts a finger to his lips and shushes me.

"We can do this the hard way if you want," he says, raising his brows at the stranger.

The drunk immediately takes his hands off my body.

"I'm not looking for trouble," he says, hands in the air.

The man in the suit beckons me to get up, so I do, and I quickly move away from the guy.

"Now. Get up and go," the stranger tells the touchy-feely drunk.

"What? Why? What did I do?" he whines.

The stranger doesn't reply. Instead, he takes off the safety.

Sweat drips down the drunken guy's forehead, and my nails dig into the leather seating.

"Leave," the guy in the suit hisses.

The drunken asshole immediately gets up and stumbles out of the seat, looking back at us a few more times before running out of the establishment.

"But he … hadn't paid the bill …" I mutter after him even though that should be the least of my worries right now. That's just how my brain works. Or that of anyone with a bunch of debt, for that matter.

"Sit."

My brain suddenly remembers the stranger with the gun, and my eyes travel to his. They're filled with rage, poisonous rage to the point that I'm left gasping for air as he speaks.

I do what he asks, and as I sit down on the opposite end of the same booth, he does so too. He places his gun on the table in front of us, but it's still pointed right at me as though he's taunting me.

"What's your name?" he asks.

Sweat drips down my back as my pulse races. "Amelia."

His lip twitches again, just like before, almost as if he wants to smile but doesn't.

"Amelia …" The way he speaks my name as though he's claiming every syllable for his own makes goose bumps scatter on my skin.

"What are you doing here?" he asks in a low, commanding voice.

I don't know why he'd ask me that … or why he'd care.

"I … I … I'm sorry, do I know you?" I mutter, confused by why this stranger with a fucking gun would save me from a dirty customer. "Please don't hurt me."

My eyes flutter back and forth between him and the gun while I contemplate my options.

He narrows his eyes at me. "Tell me what you're doing here, Amelia. *Why* do you work here?" he asks, visibly upset.

I frown. What kind of question is that? "I need to make money."

He lowers his head. "What for?"

"To pay off my loans," I spill out quickly, hoping it'll appease him.

It's quiet for some time, uncomfortably so.

His tongue darts out to wet his lips. "Don't let these fuckers touch you again."

Why would he care? Who is this guy? I thought he was trying to save me from that drunk, but now I feel as though it's more than that. It's almost as if … he wants something from me?

"You got that?" he growls.

I nod a few times.

"Good girl," he says with that same gravelly voice that makes all my senses come to life.

He rummages around in his pocket and fishes out a stack of money so thick that it makes my eyes pop. He smacks it down on the table and points at it.

"Take it."

I'm so damn confused right now. I didn't give him anything—no drinks, nothing—so what's he paying for. "Why?"

The look on his face is serious. "Take. It."

I don't think twice before I grab it and shove it in my pocket.

I mean, I'm not saying no to free money, but there has to be a catch. No one would ever give a random girl this much money without wanting something in return. Maybe this guy wants me all to himself.

I shiver at the thought. At the idea of those calloused hands that only just hovered over the trigger of his gun being gentle on my skin. At the idea of those eyes boring into mine while he'd force me to sit down with him. At the thought of his lips sliding down my neck while whispering filthy little commands into my ear, lulling me into submission.

But he doesn't.

Instead, he sneers, "Leave."

My brows furrow. "What? Why?"

"I gave you the money you'd earn tonight. Now get out of here."

I'm flabbergasted. Why would he do this? Why would he want me to go when he could have me all to himself for all this money? What would he gain from having me gone?

"Go!" he says through gritted teeth, the menacing look on his face enough to make me jolt up and run.

I don't even take the time to tell Joe that I'm done for tonight. I just rush out the door, praying that this man, whoever he is, doesn't come after me.

Because I'm certain this won't be the last time I see him.

TWO

ELI

I waited for her in the shadows of that strip joint, and when she finally appeared from behind the bar, she took my breath away. Her pretty black hair in pigtails and her petite body wrapped in a small red dress. When the men in there started looking at her like hungry wolves it made my blood boil.

No one gets to look at her like that.

No one ... not even me.

And when that fucker started touching her like he could, like he was allowed and she was there only for him, I had to intervene.

I never intervene.

This is rule number one of our House. Do not stop people from doing what they want. Observe, listen, then act.

By stepping in, I inadvertently stopped her from doing

what she needed to do, and it prevented me from seeing the truth unravel before me. The universal truth that is the basis of our very human nature—hunt or be hunted.

But I couldn't let her make that choice.

I had to step in and get that fucker to take his hands off her because I couldn't let him soil her. I couldn't allow anyone to because I wanted her all to myself.

And that is where I crossed the line.

I knew it when I first saw her in the car that I'd make this decision, and I knew then I'd end up regretting it. Because this isn't what we do, what *I* do.

I watch … I judge … I punish.

But if I succumb to lust, then I become the sinner.

Still, I cannot resist.

When she finally flees that godforsaken place after I told her to, I follow her outside. She can't be too far up ahead, maybe a couple of steps. But I trail her inconspicuously, blending into the crowd of people partying tonight in this part of town.

She walks right by them, careful not to bump into anyone even though they're all looking at her because of the way she's dressed. She didn't even grab a coat off the rails near the exit of the strip joint. That's how eager she was to leave … How scared she was of me.

It's a price I'd gladly pay to keep her out of evil's hands.

But I have to know, I need to see with my own two eyes, what she's going to do.

She skids across the pavement like she's in a hurry to get

home, her pale face even whiter than before as though she's seen a ghost. But I'm not a figment of her imagination. I'm as real as can be. She's going to wish I was merely a nightmare she could wake up from.

Suddenly, she stops in her tracks, and I wait in an alley, peeking along the building to see what she's up to.

She pauses near a homeless guy sitting on the streets holding up a tiny bowl to the people walking right by him.

But she didn't. She saw him, and she stopped.

For a split second, she looks around, so I duck behind a wall, hoping not to be seen.

When I peer at her again, she fishes the wad of cash I gave her from her pocket and stuffs it into the beggar's bowl.

The man looks up at her and smiles, but before he can say a word, she's already gone.

Whisked away by the wind like a beautiful, thoughtful, generous angel.

And it moves me.

A smile forms on my lips. "Maybe you aren't such a sinner after all, little angel," I mutter under my breath.

I didn't want to follow her, but I couldn't stop myself.

When I saw her on the streets, I knew she'd be the one.

The one I needed to have.

The one who could break me.

Never in my wildest dreams did I think she'd give that cash I gave her to a homeless man. Loans aren't easy to pay off and look at what she's willing to do to straighten out her balance. She sells her body like a whore and doesn't even mind. Still, she gives away the money I handed her freely as though it means nothing to her.

That little angel is one to keep.

One to admire. One to fear.

Goose bumps scatter on my skin just from the thought.

I know everything I need to know about this beautiful creature, this obsession of mine.

***

Amelia

On my way back home, I can't stop looking at all the cars passing by. Every time one of them stops, I feel like they're following me, or worse, that someone might step out to come and grab me.

I blow out a breath and keep walking, determined not to let the cars distract me. It's all in my mind anyway. No one's coming to get me. I didn't do anything wrong.

But then why can't I shake this feeling of imminent doom?

Because of that man at the club.

That man who pointed a gun at the head of the guy who was touching me.

It really did a number on me. Thinking about it still makes sweat pool in the small of my back.

I texted my manager that I had to leave because of an emergency. I couldn't bear to tell him the truth. What was I supposed to say? That a man with a gun threatened us and gave me a stack of cash to leave? He wouldn't believe a word.

My manager is used to fucked-up customers, but this story would take the cake. No one would pay a *waitress* to leave. Joe would probably think I didn't want to work … and I'd get fired.

I'd rather stay quiet and hope it doesn't happen again.

I swallow away the nerves as I watch some guys pass me by, and I quickly go inside the building I call home. With sweat drops rolling down my back, I step into the elevator and blow out a breath when the doors close.

Momentary safety from a turbulent world.

Just like the books I like to bury myself in.

It's such a shame they don't have more work for me at the library so I could spend all my time there instead of a mere few hours. But I guess that comes with doing what you love. You have to make sacrifices. And my sacrifice is that I have to work two jobs. One being my dream job while the other is a way to pay the bills.

When the elevator dings, I exit onto my floor and saunter to my apartment. I'm really looking forward to ditching these clothes and hopping into the shower. Just the thought brings a moderate smile to my face as I stick the keys into the lock and open my apartment door.

As I step inside, I expect the television to blast me away, but it's not turned on. Chris doesn't appear to be home even though it's late at night. Where could he be?

Going into the bedroom, I quickly rid myself of this outfit sticking to my skin and throw it in a corner. It's only then that I notice I forgot to close the curtains. I squeal and rush to the windows, covering my boobs. But as I briefly peer outside, my stomach drops, and I completely forget my own nudity.

Chris is right there in front of the building … kissing another woman.

I swallow as tears form in my eyes. I can't stop staring at the way he wraps his arms around her and gazes at her with passion in his eyes. How heavy the pang of jealousy hits me … even harder than the soul-crushing pain of losing your love to another.

The kiss he shares with her is passionate, greedy. A kiss I never dared to dream of.

The way his hands palm her back so sweetly yet so warmly, as though he wishes for nothing more than to pull her closer, makes me clutch the curtains and sigh.

This is the man I wanted but could never have.

The man he promised to be for me.

Given to another.

A scowl forms on my face, and I slam open the wardrobe and tear out the hottest dress I can find, putting it on along with sky-high heels. Then I grab the reddest lipstick from my makeup drawer and purse my lips in front of the mirror, rolling the lipstick over my own salty, teared-up lips. And after glancing at the broken woman in the mirror one final time, I throw my keys, phone, and wallet in my purse and march out the door, slamming it shut behind me.

Tears stream down my face, but he won't find me here.

***

ELI

I wait in my car and stare at the couple making out on the pavement. I'm surprised they didn't even make it to the apartment. Most people would be apprehensive to do these things in broad daylight, but not him, it seems.

I clamp a cigar between my teeth and light it, taking a big whiff before rolling down my window to take a closer look. The two just can't seem to get enough of each other, and the obscenity of their act almost makes me want to go over there and tear them apart.

Someone should teach that guy a lesson. And I think I will … after I'm done with *her*.

I blow out some of the smoke and stare at them until he finally notices me.

I cock my head at the dude as he pulls his tongue out of the woman's mouth and proceeds to stare me down in a threatening manner. But no man can easily intimidate me, especially not the likes of a disgusting pig like him.

The guy's grip on her waist softens, and he mouths something at her. She turns her head to me. The look in her eyes doesn't change one bit. I wink. She nods.

"Go," I tell the driver, and I throw the cigar onto the street.

As I roll up the window, the two stare me down until the car has long driven away. But it doesn't matter how far I drive …

Everyone will eventually catch up with their sins.

THREE

Amelia

Sixteen years ago

I can only hold one of my grandmother's hands because my other is locked tightly in a sling. The tears flow freely down my cheeks as I look at the casket being rolled out onto the streets. Six men shove it into a black car while we watch from a distance.

Everyone thought I'd be afraid of cars after what happened, but I'm not. It's not the car's fault that the road was too narrow at the bend and that we fell off a deep cliff.

I swallow hard.

There isn't much family left to mourn, just me and my grandpa and grandma. That's it.

Will my tears be enough?

If I cried hard enough, would Mommy hear it?

Would she come back?

Mommy said she and Daddy would always come back to me when they left … but she lied.

I sniff as Grandma squeezes my hand a little tighter. The second casket is rolled out of the funeral home, and my grandpa walks out too, burying a tissue deep into his pocket. Mommy once said grandparents don't ever cry because they have already cried all the tears they had, but I guess she was wrong.

Just like she was wrong when she told me she would always be here for me.

That she'd cheer me on every time I got a good grade and watch me grow old.

My heart aches as the six men load up the second casket too, and the doors are closed, the harsh sound like a slap to my face. The pain in my arm doesn't even come close to the pain in my heart.

And as the driver starts the car, and my grandparents whisk me away into theirs, I can't help but stare at the one my mommy and daddy are in right now, wondering why they're not here … and I am.

***

Present

I grab a cab to Club M, the nearest club I frequent. Tonight, I can really use a pick-me-up under a heavy bass to drown out the pain with noise and pretend everything is okay. I smile at the bouncer out front, who nods at me when I show him my ID, and then I go inside.

I look around at seats in the corners and the two staircases leading to the second floor that oversees the rest of the dance floor. Maybe I'll hang out there as I'm not in the mood for dancing, and the usual popular spot seems empty tonight.

Heading to the bar, I order a drink, then make my way upstairs. It's still busy with a bustling crowd dancing in the corner, and the couch in the back is obviously taken by a bunch of rich dudes and their posse of money-hungry girls.

I pay them no attention as I lean over the banister and wistfully stare out at the scene below, at the people dancing their night away, blissfully unaware of the emotional gash inside my heart bleeding out onto the dance floor below.

"Wishing the night away?"

I prop myself up on my elbow and look up at a man I never saw approaching from the side. A man I instantly recognize. Green eyes, smoldering look, slick dark hair, chiseled jaw. It's him.

My jaw drops, and my veins flood with adrenaline as my eyes search his. How did he get inside? Did he come here for me?

He takes a step forward. "Miss me?"

I look over the banister at the people below, but no one down there or any of the people behind me know what's happening. Everyone seems unaware of the peril I'm in … except me.

Both staircases are blocked, one by plenty of guests, and to get to the other, I'd have to pass him. And something tells me that's going to be hard, maybe even impossible.

I gulp and contemplate my options as I peer down at the crowd, wondering if I could make the jump without breaking a bone. Probably not.

"I wouldn't do that if I were you," he says, immediately drawing my attention away again.

"Who are you? Did you follow me?" I mutter, taking a step back again, my hand still clutching the railing.

His brow rises playfully. "Is that really the question you want to ask me?"

He doesn't stop getting closer, and I can't help but pull back into my shell, wondering how I'm going to escape. If I even can.

"I won't hurt you," he says, placing a hand on the banister too. "Not unless you ask me to."

My eyes immediately zoom in on the spot where he kept his gun last time, but his expensive suit covers it. He smiles and slides aside the flaps. "I'm not carrying. I didn't want to scare you, so I left it in the car."

"Too late for that." My stance grows rigid as I stop moving away and slam my lips together. "What do you want?"

He takes another step, eyeing me down as if he's testing me. To try to see if I run or if I'm up for the challenge.

I stay put, even when my heart screams for me to flee.

I cannot give another man the pleasure of winning. Not this time. Not tonight.

"What I want is irrelevant to this situation you're in ..." he murmurs.

A few fingers suddenly caressing the top of my hand tear my eyes away from his. But before I can pull my hand back, he's grabbed my wrist and pinned it to the banister.

"And your situation seems quite precarious."

"My *situation*? What are you talking about?" I taunt.

I know damn well what kind of danger I'm in when I'm near a guy like him, but I won't show that to him. The devilish smile forming on his lips tells me he's a man who enjoys that kind of thing. The hunt. The chase. Seeing a woman on her knees, begging. That type. But I'm not here to indulge him in his needs.

"With you here, it definitely is," I retort, and I try to twist myself free of his grip, but he won't let go.

"I'd beg you to think twice about who you believe is really the enemy here ..." He steps so close that I have to suck in a breath for my chest not to touch his. I can smell his cologne as he towers over me. "After all, that man at the strip club ran because of me."

"You think you're different?" I scoff, throwing a look at how he's still got ahold of me.

His grip only tightens, and he gets up close really quick. "Do not compare me to that swine." His nostrils flare. "You would let any man touch you like that, but not me."

I slap him. Hard.

And when he turns his head to me, a red mark appears on his cheek. Damn.

"I … I …" I mutter.

He grabs my only free hand and pins that to the railing too, trapping me between him and the twenty-foot drop below.

"I deserved that." His eyes narrow as he cocks his head. "You're feistier than I thought."

He leans in so far that I'm inclined backward over the edge. Panic rushes through my veins, sweat pooling on my back, as the only thing holding me back from falling is this handsome devil.

"What do you want?" I mutter.

His hand suddenly reaches for my face, and I struggle to stay put, even with one hand on the banister. His index finger and thumb slide aside a few strands of my hair until it all tumbles down over the edge, exposing my neck.

His smile broadens. "You are too beautiful. Too perfect … for him."

My pupils dilate. "Who?"

But I already know who. The question is … how does he know?

"Come on, don't play me for a fool," he replies, tilting his head so he can look at me from underneath his dark lashes. "You know as well as I do who I'm talking about."

He leans in, pressing his heavy, muscular chest against mine. His lips purse, and my eyes search for anything to look at except him … because looking at him brings fire to my body in a way no one else ever has.

His face meets mine, his stubble grazing my skin. A touch near my earlobe sends electricity all through my body.

"Say his name," he whispers.

"Chris," I mutter under my breath. "How do you know about him?"

"That's not important right now. What is important is why you know so little about him," he replies. He smiles against my earlobe. "He doesn't deserve you, and you know it."

How does this man know so much about my life? Is he a … stalker?

"Will you end things?" he asks.

My lungs suck in a breath, desperate for air even though every movement pushes me farther into him.

"Will you fight?" he asks.

Fight who? Him … or Chris?

I shake my head. "I don't understand. What do you—"

Before I can say anything else, his lips have landed on mine. It's so sudden, so violent, that I can't wrap my head around what's happening until it already is. His kiss is so subtle yet so powerful that I'm left grasping for reality. I don't know what's happening and don't know how to stop it … And I don't even know if I really want to.

Because this man's lips are like fire scorching my soul. His kiss deepens, and his hand moves from my wrist to my waist, cupping me tight to bring me closer to his body. An animalistic groan leaves his mouth, and it pushes all my buttons. The way he holds me is greedy, but his kiss is even greedier.

It's a kiss that sucks all the air out of your body without ever feeling like you need to breathe. The kind of kiss that leaves you breathless without trying. The kind of kiss you never want to stop. That happens once in a lifetime.

And this is mine.

When this man's lips slowly move away from mine to allow me a second to breathe,

the shock of what just happened overwhelms me until I remember that I already have someone to call mine. My boyfriend, Chris. Or at least he was until he kissed another woman.

And the mere thought of seeing her wrap her hands around him brings me back to reality and forces me to come face-to-face with what I've done. I'm no better than Chris.

The stranger suddenly says, "A kiss … for a kiss."

Did he just … ?

My eyes widen.

He knows.

"How?" I mutter.

"Make a choice," he says. Grabbing my hand, he pulls it to his lips, pressing a sweet, sinful kiss on top. "Him … or me."

Why would he ask me this?

His hand rises to meet my face, and he pushes aside my hair only to pause. His brows furrow as he homes in on the side of my neck.

I gasp.

The bruises.

I try to cover them up, but it's too late, and a blush spreads on my cheek.

My lips part, but he presses his finger against my mouth, stopping me from speaking. "Who did this to you?"

Panic sweeps through me once again. It's too dangerous to tell a man like him.

"I ... I ..."

His eyes rage with a fire I've never seen before. "It was him, wasn't it?" He blinks and lets go of my wrist, and for some reason, I suddenly feel cold. "It *will* end."

Before I can reply, he swirls around and walks off, leaving me breathless and completely untethered from this world.

FOUR

Amelia

After he left the club, I didn't want to go home and face Chris, so I asked my coworker Jamie if I could stay with her for the night. It was easier to run than to pretend everything was okay. Of course, Jamie asked about it, but I didn't feel like airing all my personal problems, let alone the fact that Chris was cheating on me. No, I shoved that into a corner of my mind and promised myself I wouldn't look at it again until I was ready, and she respected that.

Now I'm at work, slurping coffee like there's no tomorrow just to stay awake.

Jamie picks up a whole bunch of books and shoves them into my arms. "Can you help me sort this stack?"

It's so damn heavy my knees almost buckle.

"Uh, sure," I reply, trying to keep them from tumbling down onto the floor.

Still, one of them falls, and I try to bend over to pick it up, but then the rest of the stack almost falls too, so I stop just in time.

"Oh, stop!" Jamie says, pushing some books back onto the stack. "Don't worry, I've got it." She bends over and picks up the book from the floor, only to pause near my legs.

"Hey …" she murmurs, pointing at my knee. "You've got a nasty bruise there."

My eyes widen, and I quickly hide my leg behind the other one. "Oh, it's nothing. I just … fell down the stairs yesterday," I say, laughing it off. "It's fine."

She frowns at me as she puts the book on top of the stack in my arms. "You sure do fall a lot, don't you?"

"I bruise easily." I shrug, winking because we're both thinking of that same song now.

"Ha-ha …" She rolls her eyes. "I swear to God, Amelia, you're like a textbook bookworm, complete with the whole clumsiness."

"I know. That's why this job is so perfect for me," I reply.

"Exactly, so go, go, go!" She nudges me forward, so I take the hint and walk off before she asks any more questions that I don't want to answer.

I carry the books to the bookcase with an empty shelf that needs to be filled. I put most of them down on a table behind me so I can arrange them in the right order.

Right then, my phone buzzes, and I almost jolt from the scare. I fish it out of my pocket and see it's my own calendar reminding me it's my birthday. And I didn't get a present or any kind of happy birthday wish.

I sigh and think about Chris, wondering if he's with that woman or if he's making up ways to fix our broken relationship. Maybe he has something planned tonight. A big apology and a candlelight dinner while he grovels for forgiveness, along with a big gift for my birthday. Or maybe … nothing at all.

Maybe I prefer nothing.

Maybe nothing is better for me in the long run.

I tuck my phone back into my pocket and tell myself I'm going to celebrate it tonight, regardless if he's there or not. I don't care anymore. It's my birthday, and I'm gonna celebrate it just like I deserve, even if I have to do it all by myself.

I grab a few books off the table and turn around to place them on the shelf. I push one of them a bit too far ahead, and it tumbles off on the other side of the bookcase.

That's when a familiar set of eyes appears from behind the case. Two emerald green eyes hidden between the books, looking straight at me.

My eyes widen in shock as I cover my mouth with my hand to prevent the squeal from spilling out.

"Shh … Don't make a sound. It's a library, after all."

It's the same dark, dangerous voice from the night

before. The same guy is now standing before me mere inches away, separated only by a few books and an empty shelf.

A cold shiver turns my veins into ice.

He stares at me with that same ungodly, obsessive look.

A definite smirk forms on his lips. "Amelia …"

The way he speaks my name makes all the hairs on the back of my neck stand up.

"Have you ever had a wish?"

"A wish?" I repeat, too shocked that this is truly happening to form a cohesive answer.

"A wish that would become reality?"

I frown, baffled by his mere presence, let alone his questions.

"Amelia?" my coworker calls, and her voice distracts me enough that it makes me turn my head. Just one second. One second. That's all it took for him to pick up the book I dropped and shove it back into the empty space, covering the few inches we had to exchange looks.

I take a few steps back, expecting him to come bursting through the case with guns blazing to take me away, but nothing happens. I just stand there in blissful ignorance, wishing that it had.

Because secretly, a part deep down inside me wants to answer his question.

Wants him to show me what it could be like to live that dream.

No.

His questions were silly. The ramblings of a stranger.
A stranger who followed you to both your jobs.
Which means he knows where you live.
Shit.

Panic rushes through my veins as I throw the books onto the table and walk to the other end of the bookcase to peek along the side. But the man is already long gone. Vanished. As though he never existed to begin with and was just a figment of my imagination.

But I know for a fact that I have not gone insane.

"Amelia? Are you done? I have more." Jamie suddenly appears on the other end with a stack of books in her hands and gazes at me as though I've lost my mind. "What are you doing?" she asks.

"Oh ... um ..." I look around to make sure the man is really gone. Only one way to find out if I am going insane. "Did you see a man walk by here? By any chance?"

She frowns. "Maybe? I mean, there're a lot of them. Daily." She snorts.

"I mean just now. Did someone walk away from here?" I point at the bookcase. "Like he was standing right here."

She makes a face. "Um, I don't know? I don't keep track. Why?"

"It's nothing." I sigh and look away.

"Are you okay?" she asks.

"Yeah, yeah." I shrug it off and smile a bit, but it's a fake smile. "Sorry, I'm just a little shook, that's all."

"From a guy?" she asks as she sets the stack of books on

a nearby table. "Should I call someone? The cops?"

"No, it's fine," I say, wafting it away. "It was nothing." I snort to try to make light of it, but it still doesn't sit right with me.

"All right then, if you're sure," she replies, rolling her eyes a little. Not much, but enough for me to notice.

She must think I'm crazy. Everyone does. I'm the quiet one, the one who's always daydreaming of a better life, a bigger future. The one who's always too afraid to make the leap.

And this man … this man unchained something inside me that I didn't know existed.

Because no matter how dangerous he seemed or how much my brain was telling me to run in the opposite direction, all I wanted to do was say yes.

FIVE

Amelia

That night

The music is blaring, and I'm losing myself on the dance floor of Club M. I don't care who sees or how crazy I dance. I just need to let it all out. Let them see, let them talk; I'm done caring about what anyone thinks.

Why? Because it's my birthday, and no one cared. My grandparents have been dead for years, so they're not gonna celebrate this with me. Jamie won't either because I never told her when my birthday was. But I expected Chris to care. And now he's shown that he clearly doesn't.

So I've decided I'm not going to care anymore either.

Instead, I'm enjoying myself thoroughly while going nuts to the music, dancing the night away until my feet are tired and I'm drunk on alcohol. I don't care for a second that I'm drinking way more than usual or that this is the same club where my stalker came. I welcome the danger with open arms, or maybe it just doesn't matter at all.

The only thing that matters is me, the music, and forgetting all about my own damn birthday until it no longer exists.

And I'm loving every second of it.

***

Hours later, I wake up somewhere else entirely. I feel groggy and completely out of it. I can't even remember what I did or why I did it. I just knew I needed an escape, if only just for a moment. So I chose the alcohol to numb the pain and have a little fun all by myself.

Now, my throat hurts, and I can barely utter a sound. My whole body aches as I open my eyes and stare into the darkness surrounding me, the reality of my situation hitting me hard.

I'm not at the club … or in my apartment.

I sit up straight even though every muscle in my body hurts. I'm surrounded by trees and sitting on the grass in the middle of nowhere.

What the hell?

Where the heck am I, and how did I get here?

A searing headache slams into me, and I rub my forehead with the palm of my hand. "Ugh …" I groan.

It feels like hours have passed, but I don't remember anything.

What the hell happened to me?

The longer I think about it, the less comes into my mind. It's as if I've lost all track of time and space and forgotten everything that happened up until this point. That, or I've really hit my head hard.

All I remember is Chris … and the look on his face when I came home completely wasted …

I grab my throat and rub it, feeling exposed. But nothing I do brings back the rest of my memories. Nothing about my clothes or how I got here, or even what time it is.

I should definitely go home.

Without waiting another second, I storm off, and it doesn't take me long to realize I'm in the city park. I head straight for the nearest road. I'm shivering, and my body is freezing, but I don't give up until I've gotten back to the apartment building. By the time I'm back inside, I can barely feel my trembling body. I close the door and take a breath, trying not to panic.

But something deep inside makes me feel like something isn't right.

Even though the apartment is completely unscathed. In fact, the place looks better than how it was when I left. A little too clean, if you ask me. Did Chris do this?

I swallow as I call out, "Chris?"

But there's no response. I know he was here, but the bed is empty and hasn't been slept in.

From the open window, I spot someone leaving the building, but it isn't Chris. The figure turns around right as I peer outside, and he stares up at me while clutching his long black coat closer to his chest.

I gulp and quickly shut the curtains, breathing heavily as I hide behind them.

In that split second, our eyes connected …

And I recognized *him*.

***

With a book in my hand, I stare at the shelf in front of me. I'm supposed to put these back in place, just as I always do, but somehow, my body refuses to obey my commands. I feel so groggy, as though I've been hit by a brick. My limbs are frozen as dread floods my body, making me icy cold.

Every letter on the books in front of me scrambles into a melting pot of indescribable words, and the pages themselves are drenched in blood.

I shake my head, and the image disappears, the books back to normal as they should be.

I must be losing my mind. There's no other explanation.

I don't understand what happened to me. And after I found myself half-naked in the woods with half my memories of that night missing, I feel off. Like I'm completely off my rocker.

Something just isn't right, but I can't pinpoint what.

It doesn't help that Chris has completely disappeared off the face of the earth. I've tried texting him to no avail. He didn't even read my messages this time. I don't know what happened to him.

All I remember is being at the club, and then ... nothing.

I lost track of time and have no memory of it.

Did the alcohol hit me that hard?

Suddenly, a harsh thump makes me jolt, and I clench the book closely while I look for the noise. It was just a customer who dropped a book on the floor. No biggie. But my heart rate shot through the roof.

Why am I so panicky? I can't shake these jitters, and it's eating me up while I'm trying to work. It doesn't help that I haven't slept either, but who could when you can't even remember what you did just hours before?

"Hello, Amelia."

I hear his voice before I see his face. The mere sound makes me drop the book I was holding.

He appears from behind the bookcase, taking a step toward me.

I look around me, but there is no other way out. This bookcase is situated right against a wall.

"Don't be afraid," he says with that same sultry voice that tickles every sense of my body. "I'm not here to hurt you."

"Who are you?" I ask. "And what do you want from me?"

Every step he takes makes a clicking sound, every click pushing me closer into the wall. *Click.* He adjusts his cuffs. *Click.* My heart beats in my throat. *Click.* He towers over me, exuding pure power. Rage. Lust.

All of those things bundled into one, forcing me to cower before him.

"I'm here for you."

Panic washes over me.

"Me? Why?" My voice is barely audible.

"You don't know?" He frowns.

I shake my head thoroughly.

His eyes twitch as they narrow, and he comes even closer. "Interesting."

"I don't understand—"

Suddenly, his hand reaches for my face, the back of his index finger sliding ever so softly down my cheek, spreading goose bumps all over my body. "I can give you the one thing you've wanted but never dared to ask for." A dangerous smile spreads leisurely on his face. "True release."

Release? What does he mean?

The look on his face darkens. "Now tell me the truth."

I back away as he takes a step closer … and closer … and closer. "What truth? I don't know what you're talking about."

"Yes, you do, Amelia," he muses.

He plants a hand on the wall beside me. "I know what

you did."

I shudder in place as his energy drips over onto me, making me lose my will to fight.

I don't know why I'm overcome with the sudden urge to cry and scream, but he covers my mouth before I can.

"Shh," he whispers. "Don't want them to hear us."

"Please," I mutter through his hand.

He cocks his head. "I only want one thing from you."

Dread fills my bones, but something else is brewing underneath the surface of my skin. Something I can't describe as anything other than shame. Something I'm desperately trying to hide.

"Tell me," he says as he leans so close I can feel his breath on my skin, "your biggest secret."

My lips part, but all that exits is a choking sound.

He smiles as his hand leaves my mouth, but still, I can't utter a single word.

"You want to tell me, but you can't ... can you?" His eyes narrow, and he grabs my chin and forces me to look at him.

Tears spring into my eyes. "I don't know—"

"Yes. You. Do." That same commanding tone makes my whole body tremble. "But if you refuse to tell me, I'm going to ask you a different question: What is your darkest desire?" He plants his hand on the wall behind me again and grips my chin so firmly that I can't look away. "Your darkest wish?"

My brain is no longer in control as my heart splutters

the words before I realize what's happening. "I want to be punished."

What did I just say?

His eyes sparkle with excitement as a dirty grin spreads across his lips.

"Good little angel," he murmurs.

Before I can think about it, before I can even utter another syllable, he's already grabbed my hand and dragged me out of the library.

"Wait, I'm not done with my work yet, and I—"

He stops near a limo and opens the back door. "Get in."

I contemplate turning around and walking back inside, but something about the way he looks at me stops me. There's a possessiveness in his eyes that I can't ignore, like a warning that if I overstep, he will intervene. And I know full well what he's capable of.

So instead of fighting him, I sigh and huddle inside.

The door is shut, and the silence that follows is deafening.

What am I doing here? Why did I say those words? What the hell is wrong with me?

The door on the other side of the car opens, and he slides inside, closing it shut behind him. The locks are flicked, and he signals the driver to start the vehicle.

Fear makes me panic again.

Oh God … what did I get myself into?

"What's going to happen to me?" I ask as he turns his head toward me.

An obscene smile forms on his face, one that predicts both fury and exquisite pleasure.

"I'm going to make your wish come true."

SIX

Eli

I never imagined she'd come without a fight.

Not a single ounce of resistance as if it had all drained from her. It was as though the light had disappeared from her eyes, like snow before the sun.

All because of a few words.

Tell me your darkest secret, your deepest wish ... and I will make it come true.

I don't take those words lightly. I mean them when I say them, and I will hold myself accountable. A promise is a promise, and I don't take those lightheartedly.

Even if she might not understand the words she uttered or why.

I know.

I know everything I need to know about her, everything to make her yield.

I admit, it was part selfish desire to force her to come with me, but I couldn't just take her. No, it had to be her own choice, her own willful acknowledgment of what she needed.

Me.

"Where are you taking me?" she asks, her timid little body still trembling against the couch like a meek animal that knows it's trapped.

"You'll find out soon enough," I reply.

I press the button on the side of the door, and the barrier between the front seat and the back seat rises.

"This will only hurt for a second." I reach inside my pocket and take out a syringe. Her eyes widen at the sight of the huge needle, but it's too late for her to register what I'm doing until it's already pricked her skin.

She shrieks, but the sound quickly dies out after the drugs course through her system.

She might not know me, but she'll know the real me soon enough.

I'm the one who's going to make her beg.

***

Amelia

When I come to, my head feels as though I've been hit with a hammer when I know that isn't true. My ears are ringing, and my eyes are stuck together. I'm so groggy I don't even know how much time has passed since I fainted.

Since I was … drugged.

It all comes flooding back into my brain. The man who followed me and watched me in the library. The man who made me tell him a secret … a dark wish that had been looming in the back of my mind …

Punish me.

My eyes burst open, and my lungs fill with oxygen as I lean up to peer at my surroundings. I'm in a huge room that I've never seen before on a luxurious red velvet bed that's too cozy for my own good. None of this feels right.

How did I get here?

Then it hits me. That man …

I grab my arm.

I can still feel the puncture wound from the needle. There is a bandage covering it.

My stomach suddenly does a one-eighty, forcing me to throw the blanket off and hurl over the edge of the bed. Fuck. I've never felt more nauseous in my life.

Suddenly, the door opens, and in walks a girl with a tray

filled with pill bottles and a cup of water. She immediately puts it down on a dresser near the door.

"Oh, no …" she mutters. She grabs a towel hanging from a hook near the door and walks toward me. I lean back against the bed and crawl away from her, curling my knees up to my chest in order to appear small. Meek. Not worthy to start a fight with.

This is what I've always done to ward off any attackers. I am not the proud lioness fighting to defend herself. I'm the roadkill that pretends it's dead so it doesn't get caught.

But so far, that strategy has failed. Big time.

So I grab the nearest object I can find, a lamp, and hold it up like some sort of shield.

The girl raises her hand in surrender. "I won't hurt you. I promise."

I stare at her as my heart races out of my chest. I don't know who she is or if I can trust her. I don't even know where I am or how I got here.

"I'm just gonna clean this up," she says, still moving slowly as though I'm some kind of animal that could attack at any moment.

Maybe I am. Right now, with all these drugs leaving my body, I don't know what I'm capable of, and neither does she. All I know is that guy drugged me, and now I'm stuck in some bed. God only knows where I ended up.

The girl cleans up the carpet with the towel before spraying it over. Not once does she raise a brow or wince at the fact that I soiled the floor.

I peer over the edge of the bed to look at how meticulously she works, rinsing every nook and cranny. "Don't worry about it," she says as she looks up at me. "This always happens."

Always? As in … this has happened to other people?

Oh, God.

"The drugs should be wearing off," she says, and she places the pills and some water on the nightstand beside me. "You should feel better in a couple of minutes after you take these."

She sounds as if she knows exactly what she's talking about, and I don't doubt that for a second. But I won't take these meds, not even if my life depends on it. It's not worth the risk of getting poisoned.

She rinses the towels and tucks them in a bin. "I'll come pick up the dirty laundry later, okay?"

I don't reply, don't even move an inch. I just stare at her as she smiles and then leaves the room. Finally, I allow myself to breathe again.

What the fuck, what the fuck, what the fuck?!

I put the lamp down and throw the blanket off, stepping over the stain I just made. I don't even care about the mess. All I care about is finding out where the hell I am and why this man brought me here.

Suddenly, the door opens again, and I stumble into the bed, trying to grab ahold of something in order not to fall.

It's that same girl again, and she clears her throat. "Sorry, I forgot to mention something important."

I look up at her, and without waiting for her to say more, I ask, "Where am I?"

Her lips part as though she's about to say something, but then she changes her mind, and says, "House of Sin."

House of Sin? What is that?

"He expects you to be dressed and ready for him."

Before I can ask any more questions, she closes the door on me.

"No, wait!" I stagger to the door and bang on it hard, but there is no reply. The door is locked, and no matter how often I pull the handle, it won't budge.

But I won't give up. "Please! You've got to let me out! This is a mistake!"

I keep banging on the door until my hands hurt and my body feels heavy.

"Please, let me out!" I beg. "I don't want to be here!"

But deep down, I already know it's futile.

I sink to the floor, my hand still on the wood, as I disappear into my mind for a moment to try to cope with things and make sense of my new reality. The realization that I'm trapped in a room I don't belong in hits me hard, and tears well up in my eyes. It's as if I'm stuck in a nightmare I can't seem to wake up from.

All because of that man ... that man who stalked me to my work and took me against my will. And I don't even know his name.

I stare at the room around me, wondering what the hell I'm supposed to do other than dress myself. I'm not even sure I really want to, but do I really have a choice? If I don't, would they let me out of this room?

Just thinking about being stuck here forever gives me the creeps. I mean, it's not an ugly room. The décor is actually luxurious, with a soft velvety couch on the side, a big bookcase filled with books, and a giant wardrobe. But the windows are barred. This place is nothing but a glorified prison, and I'm being kept here like some sort of criminal.

What did I do to deserve this?

Nothing ... nothing I can remember, that is.

All I know is that when he asked me what my darkest wish was, I told him I wanted to be punished. It just slipped out. I didn't know it would lead to me being taken and put into an expensive cage.

I sigh to myself and get up from the floor. No point in hanging around and doing nothing. So I gather my courage and inspect every nook and cranny of my room, trying to find an exit, a hidden compartment, or anything that could lead me to either a key or a way out.

But the longer I search, the more despair takes over. I find nothing, absolutely nothing.

"Fuck!" I growl out loud, slamming my fists onto the barred windows.

Nothing's left unscathed. I even searched under the bedding and peeled away some of the wallpaper. There's nothing I can use to force my way out. My hand rests against the window, but my view is blocked by the rain splashing down from above.

Guess there's no other choice.

I turn my gaze toward the big wardrobe in the corner next to me. I open it up, expecting rage to further fuel my need to rip it all apart. Instead, my jaw drops at the beauty in front of me. Several glittery gowns with amazing colors, laced in diamonds and chiffon, are hanging in the wardrobe. Gowns from several high-end brands that only a princess would wear. But I am no princess, and I refuse to play this game.

So I grasp the smallest, most mediocre and modest dress I can find; a short nude dress with no embellishments and a tight fit around the legs and neck. He will expect me to get dressed. Well, that girl never said he'd expect me to dress fancy.

With a smug grin on my face, I take off my clothes and glare at them for a second. These were the jeans and crop top I was wearing when I was working at the library when he came for me, and when I look at them, all I see is his daunting face and those green eyes gazing right back at me as though they could peer into my soul.

Shivering in place, I throw the clothes in the corner. I grab the only pair of panties from the drawer and put them on, then the dress. It fits me snugly and feels like the perfect size … as though it was made just for me.

I inspect myself in the mirror and smile at the woman in front of me, but the smile is fake, empty, emotionless. A woman who's going through the motions expected of her while screaming on the inside. But then why does it feel like

I can't let it all out?

Suddenly, there is a knock on the door, and I hold my breath.

The door opens. First, a foot is visible. Then the black suit. Another foot. The man with the square jaw steps inside my room again, his thin lips tugging at the corner into a rugged, crooked smile.

I freeze in place as he closes the door behind him. The click of the lock falling into place makes my heart jump. Every step he takes is another one that forces me to stay put, as though his very presence is enough to make my body falter. My muscles fail to listen to me when I tell them to move. When I want to raise a fist and punch him for daring to get close.

Instead, I just stand there, gazing at both of us in the mirror, wondering why he did all of this to me … and what he's planning to do.

As he walks closer, I hold my breath until I can practically feel his body against mine. He looks at me through the mirror, his tongue darting out briefly like a wolf would when it's about to eat.

"You look … beautiful," he says, his voice luscious, almost sexy. "Peculiar choice of dress, but I can appreciate that," he muses, and he places a hand on my shoulder. Goose bumps scatter on my skin. "Look at yourself … So pretty yet so violent, those thoughts swirling inside your head."

I spin on my heels, forcing his hand to drop from my

shoulder. Even though my heart is racing, I come face-to-face with the man who trapped me.

"Who are you?"

That same dark, almost hungry smile appears. "Call me Eli."

Eli … such an innocent name for such a devilish man.

"What do you want from me?" I ask.

"What do *I* want?" He snorts, almost as if to laugh at me. "No, Amelia. This is what *you* wanted."

My eyes widen as fire rages through my chest. "What I wanted? I never asked to be locked up like some pet."

Suddenly, his hand is on my neck, fingers twisted around my flesh, causing me to gasp. "You asked …" His grip loosens, and his thumb caresses me so softly it confuses the hell out of me. "And I am here to make your wish come true."

Tears well up in my eyes from my predicament. "What do you plan on doing to me?"

He cocks his head and bites his bottom lip, his eyes glazing over my body as though he's taking in all that he owns. "Whatever I choose … Because that's what you asked for: To be punished."

"I take it back," I say as a tear rolls down my cheek.

His hand slides up my neck, gently caressing my face until he reaches my cheek, where he picks up the lonely tear with his index finger and studies it for a moment. "Too late."

He grabs my hand, lifting it. My eyes close, expecting

pain.

But I'm surprised by a gentle kiss on the top of my hand. His rugged lips feel hot on my skin, and turmoil breaks my heart in two. This handsome stranger has taken me into what I assume is his home, but it's cost me my freedom. All because of that one question he asked me.

His lips part again. "I will see you tonight."

Then he turns around and marches off, leaving me with nothing except more insufferable questions that I don't know the answers to.

SEVEN

ELI

When the door closes behind me, my fists finally relax. I was so close, so damn close to just taking her right then. She looked ripe, ready for the taking. So picture perfect in front of that mirror that I wanted nothing more than to caress her. Even with that modest dress she chose, an obvious statement that didn't elude me, I still wanted to claim her. Grab her. Take her. Fuck her into oblivion.

But I know I have to wait. These things must happen the way they're supposed to. The way my father taught me.

Punishments are to be carried out in an effective manner while following the rules. It is the only way this arrangement will work. The sinner is punished while the punisher sins.

And judging by my own tented pants, I'm certain I've already started. I gaze down at my pants, willing my cock to go down. Soon.

Just a few more hours … and then she'll be mine.

***

Fifteen years ago

Sandwiches, snacks, and cups of coffee and juice fill the table in front of me, but my stomach turns at the thought of eating or drinking any of it.

My hands are sweaty as they briefly touch the table to find something to hold on to.

I feel uneasy, weak to the bone.

I've never felt like this before.

Not even after all the many trips my father took to foreign lands, only to return with strangers I'd never met before and would never see again.

Or when my father disappeared for days on end, forcing the staff to take care of me like I was their child, only to come back out of his basement that I'm forbidden from entering.

And not even when my mother told me she had never really wanted me.

None of those made me feel the way I do now. It's like my nerves are shutting down, buzzing slowly as they stop sensing anything around. No matter how many times someone pats me on the shoulder or offers me a fake smile or a hug, nothing registers.

All I can do is stare at this frame standing on the table

next to me, a hand-painted picture of my mother. The way her hand rests on her lap as though she's comfortable in her place. But she never was.

Her eyes always skittish, her body always frail to the touch. Every time I came too close, she would shoo me away. I always thought it would go away with time, but the longer it lasted, the worse it became until she no longer wanted to see me at all.

And then she got her wish granted.

I sigh out loud while glancing at her urn, whispering a wish to myself that I'd never say out loud.

"You want her to stay dead forever?"

Wide-eyed, I spin on my heels, my hand rising to meet this new threat as I'm overcome with rage.

But the petite frame of a little girl stops me midair, her doe-like eyes blinking at me as though she doesn't even know the magnitude of her question. She cocks her little round head, her black hair framing her face as her pink cheeks grow bigger from the cute smile that appears on her face.

"You shouldn't wish for those things."

I frown, grinding my teeth. "How would you know?"

She fishes her tiny wallet from her pocket and takes out two small pictures tucked away, rubbing her lips together. "I keep them here with me always. Even when they're not there."

I swallow and clutch the table behind me. "You lost a parent?"

She rubs her lips together and looks down at the floor while sticking up two fingers.

"Both?" I suck in a breath. "Wow. I'm sorry."

"It's okay … It's been a year now."

"Still, sounds rough," I reply as I look down at my own feet, thinking about what I did. "Especially because they loved you."

I said those words out loud. Even when I knew I shouldn't, I said them anyway because that's what I felt deep down. Because knowing my mother has been more painful than I think not knowing her would have been.

Suddenly, the girl grabs my hand. The touch is subtle but intense. Like an earthquake underneath your own two feet that no one else can feel, shaking you to your core.

And instead of pulling away, like I always do when someone tries to touch me, I freeze and let the warmth of her touch overcome me. The rage coiling around my heart, squeezing it tight, releases its grip, if only for a second until the little girl lets go again.

"I'm sorry," she says.

Sorry.

Like it could erase the pain.

Like she even knows me.

Yet these words of this strange kid make me feel something for the very first time since I came to this funeral home.

"Even if you hated your mom …" she adds. "She didn't deserve to die."

I lower my eyes as my hair falls over like a curtain to hide my shame as my hands form fists. "I didn't hate her." The silence is thick between us as the others mingle and talk, but our silence says more than their words ever could.

"She hated *me* for existing," I say through gritted teeth.

"Maybe she was just scared and confused," the girl replies. "Maybe she had all these emotions swirling through her head, just like you, and she didn't know what to do with them, so she said something she didn't mean."

Maybe. Maybe not. Who even knows? No one. I tried so many times to understand her, but she always pushed me away. And my father? He refused to talk about her.

"It doesn't matter," I say, balling my fist. "She's dead now. Gone. And they're all talking and eating like it's the most normal thing in the world."

"They don't understand," the girl says, looking at the crowd. "But I do." She looks back up at me, that same sparkle in her eyes that she had when she first laid eyes on me. "You're not alone."

I turn away, rolling my sleeves up, and growl, "I am."

Her eyes flicker down to my arms, pupils dilating, and it dawns on me what she's looking at. The bruises. Shit. How did I forget so quickly? I cover them up again even though I know it's too late.

She grabs my arm. "Who did that?"

I don't answer.

"Was it her?"

"No," I bark, wishing I never showed them. "She never

even touched me!"

She takes a step back, rubbing her lips together. "So it's your dad."

I don't respond. I don't see the point.

"It's okay to be mad."

"I have to stay strong," I reply, fighting the anger. "That's what my father always says."

"And sometimes parents lie," she says. "Mine told me they'd always come back to me, but they never did." She steps forward again and grabs both my hands. "I think you just need a friend."

I lick my lips and hide the tears forming in my eyes, forcing them to stay at bay. "I don't need anyone."

"Yes, you do," she says. "We all need someone to talk to. To hug."

And she steps forward and wraps her arms around me. My whole body begins to tremble. This girl, who is almost half my age, makes my legs almost cave in on me. And her sudden attachment moves me, stripping me bare of all I thought I knew.

"It'll be okay."

At this moment in time, when the world I thought I knew crumbles before me, she is there to keep me grounded and tell me things will be okay. Even if they won't, even if they never can … a tiny sliver of me wants to believe because she says so.

Because she's here for me when no one else is.

"Amelia!"

She suddenly lets go of me and turns around to look at a lady with gray hair tucked in a bun, the skin around her cheeks sagging so much she reminds me of a bulldog. I recognize the woman from the news. Wife to a very powerful man, one who plays politics. A friend of my father's. Did they raise her after her parents died?

"Are you coming?" the lady calls.

I guess that's a yes.

She nods and then turns to face me one last time. "Hate is a sin. Did you know?" She smiles. "My grandma told me. Sins never do anyone any good."

"Your grandma is right," I reply, and even though I don't want it to, a smile still tugs at my lips. "But I'm not here to be good."

"Sure you are," she replies, grabbing my hand one last time. "Everyone is. You just have to believe in yourself."

When she lets go, it feels as though the light leaves with her.

And for the first time in my life, I feel like chasing that very same light until it blinds me from the darkness in this world.

EIGHT

Amelia

Present

My hand still tingles from his kiss. All I can do is stare at the skin on the top of my hand, wondering when the sensation will disappear. But the longer I look, the heavier it feels, as though his very essence penetrates my skin.

Enraged, I rub my hand against my dress in an effort to erase his mark. Why would he kiss me? Why would he confuse me like that?

He's my captor, a man who took me without asking me if I wanted to be here. And I couldn't even fight him. In fact, when his lips touched my skin, for a moment, a spark of lightning surged through my body, heating me up from within.

And I hate it. I hate it more than anything, more than the wealth in this room, more than these opulent dresses, the expensive furniture, and the diamond earrings and necklaces hanging from the boudoir.

None of this is real. It just can't be.

I pace around the room while my mind swirls with turbulence, and I lash out at anything and everything around me. I rip apart the bedding, tip over the dressing table, and pull everything out of the wardrobe.

When my rage subsides, all that's left is ragged breaths and salty tears streaming down my face. I stare at myself in the mirror, at the broken girl in the nude dress, doing what her captor wants just so she'll be treated right.

Why didn't I fight? Why didn't I try to escape?

The door was open. I could've run.

But who knows what lies beyond this room. How many guards are stationed outside, waiting to grab me?

This man must be rich and powerful beyond my imagination for him to be able to afford all of this luxury for a mere prisoner.

But I don't understand why he set his eyes on me. Why he made me the target of his obsession.

I thought if I mulled about it long enough, it would come to me. That I would be able to dig into my own brain and find out why I said those words … why I asked him to punish me.

But the longer I think about it, the less I understand my

own motives, let alone his.

None of this makes sense.

It's like I'm in the middle of a nightmare I can't wake up from.

A nightmare that began the first time I saw *him*.

All I can do to pass the time is read and watch TV, but that gets boring fast when there are only old cable networks, and I've already read more than half of the books here.

At night, someone knocks on my door. I sit up in my bed with curiosity, still wearing that stupid dress, expecting it to be him. Instead, it's that same girl who first came into my room to clean up the mess I made and give me some pills. She looks at the nightstand for a brief second, the pills still there as a stark reminder that I don't trust her or anyone else in this house.

She clears her throat and brings in a tray filled with food that immediately draws my attention away from the mistrust and forces me to remember my own growling stomach.

"I hope you're hungry," she says as she places the tray on a table near the door. "The cooks made this especially for you."

Cooks? So the guy is rich, after all.

"If you have any special dietary wishes, please let me know."

Dietary wishes? What is this, a restaurant?

"Nothing too special, just … if you have allergies or anything." The way she tucks her hair behind her ear reminds me of myself. "Well, bon appetit."

When she opens the door again, I say, "Wait."

She pauses for a moment. It's my only chance.

"Who is that man? Eli? And what does he want from me?"

"Eli merely wants to give you what he wants to give all of his guests," she explains. "Peace."

"Peace?" I frown, confused.

She touches her temple. "Peace of mind."

That makes no sense at all, and I fold my arms in protest. "Drugging someone and then locking them up in your house? That's one heck of a way to give someone peace of mind."

She doesn't blink. She just stares at me as if our conversation doesn't even faze her. "Eli does what he has to do to give you what you need."

What he has to do?

As she steps out, one foot already outside the door, I call out again. "Wait! Why did he do this? Why me?"

She glances at me over her shoulder. "Ask him."

Then she closes the door. I groan and fall back onto the bed. They're all so cryptic and never actually answer any of my questions with any explanations. It's like no one wants me to understand. Or maybe they think I won't. But then why am I here? He told me this was my punishment, but what does that even mean? What kind of disciplining does he have in mind, or is being locked in here my punishment?

Not to mention that I don't even know what I'm being punished for. Or why I asked for it in the first place.

I rub my eyes in annoyance and then sit back up again. No point in pondering when nothing can give me answers. Not until he comes back anyway, which I'm sure he will. And I'm going to need all the energy I can get to deal with him.

So I sit down at the table and look at the tray. It's filled with plates of delicious food—rump steak with sauce, baked and salted potatoes with thyme, and a few veggies covered in cheese.

I pick up the fork, my stomach protesting against my anger. But a note underneath the cutlery makes me stop in my tracks. I pick it up and read it.

Eat. Be ready. Tonight.
Eli

The fork in my hand shakes as I try to control my fear, rage, and tears. They all hit at once like a wave crashing into the beach. The food in front of me suddenly doesn't look so appetizing anymore.

I am giving this man what he wants by eating this. So I shove away the tray and sit down on the bed again, forcing my stomach to curb its appetite. Even though the sweet aromas are tempting, I will not give in. If this will displease him, then so be it. At least I stood my ground. If I'm too frozen to speak or move, at least this way I can show him I don't intend to play along with this charade.

He's going to tell me exactly why I'm here and what he

plans to do with me. And then I'll see what options I have to get out of this mess.

After waiting for what feels like hours, someone knocks on the locked door.

"Come in," I mutter, but I doubt they'd wait for me to reply.

The door handle is pushed, and in steps that same guy. Eli. The man who took me from the comfort of that library I love so much into this gilded cage.

I don't know why he knocks when I'm not the one who decides if he comes in or not. I don't have a key … he does, so all of this is just formalities, a nicety to make me believe I have power when I have none. My freedom literally rests in the palm of his hands.

And now I'm going to have to beg to get it back.

***

ELI

When I close the door behind me, she tenses up, which is exactly what I'd expect from a girl like her. Like a lost doe, she's still willing to fight as though it would ever give her an inkling of a chance to escape.

I gaze at the food that remains untouched on the table. A smirk spreads on my lips.

"You haven't eaten," I say.

She doesn't reply. Of course not. Who would when there's a monster standing in your room?

That's what she thinks of me, and it clearly shows on her face.

But I am not the monster here … she is.

She just doesn't know it.

But she will … soon. It's only a matter of time.

They all succumb to this place, and she is no exception, no matter how much she thinks she is. The harder she fights, the easier it is to get to her.

But I will start slowly … there's no rush with perfection.

I step in closer, and her fingers instinctively curl up the bedding underneath her. Each step I take makes her push herself back across the bed until there's no more room, and she's stuck against the wall.

I sit down on the bed beside her, watching her chest rise and fall with each heavy breath, as though she's contemplating whether to try to escape. But the door is locked, and no one has the key except me. And I know she knows this. Her eyes already found it the minute I stepped into this room and tucked that key into my pocket. And if she wants it, she knows she's going to have to either fight me … or beg.

And I think we both already know which option she's going to choose.

I hold out my hand, but she inches back and grabs the blanket, covering herself with it as though she intends to hide from me.

"Don't be scared. I won't bite," I say, adding a gentle smile.

"Why are you doing this to me?" she asks.

"You know why."

I cock my head and scoot a little closer until she can no longer crawl back. I reach over to the blanket she's clutching and slowly drape it down her body until her beautiful dress is shown to me again.

"You don't have to hide from me. I won't hurt you."

She shivers in place, and her eyes flutter from the key in my pocket to my eyes and back again, almost like an injured animal contemplating what to do.

"You won't get this key," I say, lowering my head to meet her gaze. "And if you do, the guards will stop you from escaping."

She swallows, and the look on her face changes from determined to hopeless in a matter of seconds. A pure delight to witness.

"What do you plan on doing with me? Are you just going to keep me here like some pet?" she asks.

"Perhaps." I raise my brows. "Or maybe I am not as evil as you think I am."

"You stole me away from my home," she says through gritted teeth.

"I took you because you asked me to," I reply, and I lean in to grab her chin. "And don't ever think I will forget that."

She jerks her head out of my soft grip and looks the

other way as though it will give her power just to spite me. But I cannot let my arrogance get to me and let her control the narrative.

"This will be your home for now," I say, firmly planting my hands on my knees. "And you will do as you're told."

"Why?" she asks. "Why should I?"

"Do not test me, Amelia," I retort, the harshness in my tone enough to make her soften her look. "I may look like a gentle man, but I am far from it. I will break you if I have to."

"Break me? But I didn't do anything," she exclaims.

"You didn't?" I raise a brow at her, which makes her pupils dilate. "Or is it just that you can't remember?"

Her body begins to quake. "What are you talking about?"

"You *knew* you needed punishment … but you don't know *why*." I lean into her and place a hand on the bedding beside her. "Curious, don't you think?"

Her lips quiver. "You're lying."

"I wish I was, little angel." I grab a loose strand of her hair and tuck it behind her ear. "But you are a sinner."

"Tell me what I did then," she hisses.

I smile again. "If I told you, you wouldn't believe me," I say, cocking my head as my finger lingers on her cheek. "But you will learn when you're ready."

"I don't believe you," she murmurs, but the tears welling up in her eyes tell me that's a lie.

"You keep telling yourself that. Maybe you'll believe it

eventually," I say.

She makes a tsk sound. "Did you just come here to gloat?"

"No. I came here to explain how this is going to work," I say, and I lean away again and stretch my fingers, cracking my knuckles. She keeps her eyes on me, but her body is much less defensive than it was before. "You're in my house now, and I expect you to behave. You will shower or bathe every day and dress appropriately, or as requested. You will eat when offered food. You will dine with me when I demand it."

"Why? Give me one good reason I'd do any of that," she retorts.

My eyes lock onto hers. "You will have to earn your freedom."

Her nostrils flare as her lips part.

"And I think you know exactly what that entails," I add, and I place my hand on her knee.

She shudders in place, her body instantly clenching. But she doesn't say no. She doesn't even try. And I admire that.

I lift my head and stare at the beautiful paintings on the ceiling. "You must repent for your sins." When my head lowers again, my eyes find hers, and a hunger grows inside me. "To me."

NINE

Amelia

I'm no longer shaking, but my body has frozen over like I've dipped my toes straight into frigid lakes of the underworld.

A single tear rolls down my cheek, and his hand rises to brush it away. "You must do what I want, when I want. Because I know what you did."

So he's blackmailing me. And for what? Something I can't remember?

"How do I know you're telling the truth?" I say.

He smiles but it's a crooked, dangerous smile. "Angel, your mind already knew," he says with an almost saint-like voice. "That's why you confessed that you need punishment."

My jaw tightens when he briefly brushes my chin with his index finger.

I wish I could bite him. That I had the guts to punch him, kick him, flee for my life. But I don't. I'm frozen to the bed like some fragile doll, waiting to be used. Because deep down, I know there's no use in fighting him.

I could never win. And even if I did, guards behind that door would be waiting to grab me, so what's the point?

He gets up from the bed and stands tall before me, like a shadow looming over me. "If you want to be free again, you must pay for it with your sins."

How could this man who first appeared like such an elegant gentleman when he talked to me at the library be such a devil in disguise?

"And you can guarantee I will be free again if I do what you want?" I ask.

I don't want to entertain this thought, but I have to know what's on the other end. What will happen if I agree … if I let him do what he wants to me …

He nods. "But only once you've been punished for your sin."

My sin. The way he says it, like it's some godforsaken crime, like I've done something inhumane, angers me. I'm not that type of girl. I always obeyed the rules, listened to my teachers, and respected my parents. So wherever he is getting this from is beyond me.

A shiver runs through me the moment I look into his hawk-like eyes.

There's no possible way to get out of this room. Not without his help. I'm going to have to win his trust first before I can even think of escaping.

I swallow and sit up straight on the bed, lowering my legs onto the floor so my feet are right in front of him. I look up into his dark, sultry eyes and find them filled with something indescribable, like a ... hunger.

A hunger I've only seen before in customers at the strip club.

Is that ... what he wants from me? My body?

I swallow away the lump in my throat as I gaze up into his eyes, wondering what goes on beyond them, what he's thinking about when he stands here humiliating me over something I can't remember I did. Something I don't know I ever even did.

But if it's this or staying in this room forever, I think I already know which one I'd pick. So I sit before him and spread my legs, opening them wide. His eyes peer down between them, his Adam's apple moving up and down as his pants strain.

All men are the same. Even the most chivalrous gentlemen hide inner beasts that wish to devour. And this wolf has set its eyes on me.

Lifting my hand, I grab his zipper, but before I can pull it down, he's caught my wrist. He firmly twists my hand away from his tented pants.

"No, angel," he says, his grip so tight that it almost hurts. "I will decide how this is done."

Of course, a man like this would refuse to give up any power, even if it promises pleasure.

I cock my head and lean in even closer. "Wanna use me? Fuck me? Just like all the other men in my life?"

His nose twitches, and his lips grow even thinner than before.

Suddenly, he lunges at me and grabs both my hands, pinning me to the bed while crouching on top of me.

"You think this is a game?" he growls.

"To you, it is," I hiss.

I know he doesn't like that I know how these things go, how men like him are. I can see it in his eyes, the rage building and building until it's about to explode. But I can't help myself. It's the only way I've learned how to fight back. Not with strength but with emotion. If I cannot run, at least I can try to unravel my captor. Like a puzzle I need to put together to decode the grand scheme and make my escape.

However, before I can say anything else, he's dragged me up the bed and reached behind the boards for a pair of cuffs that he attaches to my wrists, locking me in place.

He leans back up on his knees and gazes at me as if to admire his work.

"Shouldn't talk back to me like that, angel," he murmurs. "You will stay here until you've learned your lesson."

"What? But I didn't do anything," I reply, jerking on the cuffs, but it's no use. They're tightly chained to the bed.

He plants both his hands on the headboard beside my

head and leans over to glare at me from up close. His dreamy eyes wide, dark but inviting, like a siren's call luring me into submission, but I won't fall for that trap. I look away, angered that he'd take even more of my freedom by trapping me on this bed.

"You think you didn't ... but the mind can be a treacherous thing." A devilish smirk forms on his lips, and he grabs my chin and forces me to look at him. "But I will help you."

"Help?" I scoff. "All you've done is take more away from me."

He nods. "And I will keep taking more ..." He leans in closer until I can feel his breath on my skin. "And more ..." His lips linger near my ear, whispering sweetly like a man drunk on the possibilities. "And more. Until you have nothing left to give, and even then ..." His lips curl. "More." That last word almost comes out with a wolfish growl, and it manages to make goose bumps scatter on my skin.

He smiles against my earlobe, his lips grazing my skin, tantalizing my senses as my body betrays me. I knew he was handsome the very first time I saw him, so handsome that it made me stop in my tracks and stare. When he's this close, I can't deny it does something to me, but being attractive won't hide his sadistic ways.

"I don't use ... I don't fuck ..." The way he pronounces each word so carefully as though he wants me to linger on them like I would on a kiss makes me swallow hard. "I teach."

I gulp. "Teach what?"

Pain? Anger? Fear?

"Humility," he growls. His tongue dips out to drag a line from my ear to my cheek, where he leans away to look me in the eyes again. "Tell me … what did you think would happen when you provoked me like that?"

"You think that just because you call me angel I'll be good? That I'm easy?" I hiss, trying to keep my resolve even though it's crumbling fast, knowing that I'm locked in his chains.

"Easy? No." He bites his bottom lip, and for some reason, my eyes home in on it. "Willing … yes."

I frown. "I didn't—"

He plants a finger against my lips and says, "You asked." His eyes narrow as his hand slides down my thigh, my body twisting and contorting so I don't feel the heat rising in my belly or have to face the wetness pooling between my legs when he gets closer and closer.

"And now it's time for you to beg."

He takes his hand away and crawls off the bed, leaving me breathless, filled with an unwanted desire I can't place and wish I could rinse off.

He steps away and fishes something from his pocket, a tiny device with a few buttons on it.

I frown. "What is that? What are you going to do?"

He bites his lip again and looks at me with a certain type of delight that I can only describe as vicious. "What you deserve."

He pushes the button, and suddenly, everything in my body begins to vibrate.

"What the…?" I mutter, trying to keep it together.

But then he cranks it up a notch, and I'm practically vibrating across the bed. Only the cuffs keep me in place. The more I focus, the harder it becomes, and it's only then that I realize where the vibrations are coming from.

My panties.

"Fuck," I growl, trying to jerk my way out of these chains, but it's no use. I'm stuck here, left to his mercy, and his mercy has long disintegrated. I don't understand. They were just panties. "How did you—"

"Your panties are lined with a special kind of vibrating pad that only activates on my command." He holds up the device with the buttons and tosses it in the air. "Handy little thing, if you ask me."

"How dare you," I growl.

"I didn't do anything … you put those panties on," he says, pointing at my legs, making me hyper aware of the fact that he can see me squirm. "You've got no one to blame but yourself."

I swear, he raised the intensity again, but I can't tell. I can barely look at him without wanting to moan, and I hate it.

"That's it … feel the delicious shockwaves forcing you to come to terms with your captivity," he says, taking delight in the fact that I'm strapped to the bed.

"You're enjoying this, aren't you?" I clutch my legs together, trying to keep the pleasure at bay, but it only makes it harder.

He smiles. "I try not to … After all, this is your punishment."

This is my punishment? That means … "So you'll let me out after this is over?"

"Over?" He laughs so diabolically that it makes me want to look away. "We're only just beginning."

I gasp in shock as he turns around and walks off. "No, wait!"

"Good luck and try not to come too many times. I'd like you to save some for me."

He marches out and closes the door behind him but not before pushing the button so many times to increase the intensity that the last thing he hears coming from my mouth is a long-drawn-out moan echoing through my room.

TEN

ELI

The moment I left her there, all by herself, simmering in her own rage and desire, I knew I'd made the right decision. She's going to make a great pet. At least, for as long as I'll have her under my wing. I don't know how long that will be yet, but it depends on her, not me. She may think otherwise, but I am not the one who chose this. She did.

She asked me to punish her, so I will, no matter how much she resists. No matter how much she pretends she doesn't want it, she said those words for a reason. And it is my job to make her realize why.

I readjust my fly after listening to her moan out loud again. I did not want to toy with her yet, but her incessant need to question my motives and my character gave me no choice. I don't take kindly to girls thinking they can one-up me. The more she fights, the more she tries to wriggle her way under my skin, the more I will force her to submit and obey.

Eventually, she'll understand. Maybe not now … but it won't take long with those vibrating panties clinging to her pussy, forcing her to come and come and come until she's lost track. I should've told her to count. I smirk from just the thought, but somehow, my cock pushes back against the fabric of my pants too. It can't help but react to the sounds she's making. Normally, it wouldn't faze me, but this girl … this girl is something else. From the moment I spotted her, I knew she was perfect and that she'd make it hard on me, but I like a challenge.

Still, I have to admit when she asked me if I was going to fuck her, the possibility did briefly pass through my mind. She looked so beautiful in that nude dress, ripe and ready for the taking. And the way she arched her neck when my lips grazed her skin almost made me want to kiss her right there and then.

She's already gotten under my skin, but I won't let her notice that. No, even when she was squirming and mewling underneath me, I forced myself to stop when I so desperately wanted to take what I wanted from her.

And that … that is my sin.

Tasting the fruit is forbidden if it doesn't serve a purpose, which is why I've made it my life's mission to use my desire. Lust isn't the objective. It's a tool to gain access to the most private parts of a person's soul. And once they've given that up … they're done for.

I rummage in my pocket and press the button to up the vibrations once more, and her moans are audible all the way from the staircase. A devilish smile forms on my lips. Oh, little angel ... when this is all over, you're going to beg for more.

***

Amelia

I don't know how many hours passed, but it's enough to make me want to faint. I've had so many orgasms that I've lost count. Each as overwhelming as the next, but none as bad as the ones that happened after the vibrations were upped again and again. Even when I thought it couldn't get worse, Eli proved me wrong, and it's driving me insane with lust.

What if it won't end? What if he'll keep me in these panties forever? Strapped to this bed like a doll he can use whenever he wants?

The mere thought makes me burst into tears. I wish I'd never put on these foul clothes. That I hadn't given in to the idea of more freedom so easily, because now it's come back to bite me in the ass. The more I give, the more he's willing to take ... but at what cost? My sanity?

I writhe around on the bed, which is soaked with my pussy juices, hoping I could wriggle my way out of this mess. But no matter how hard I try, I can't shake off these panties. They're too tightly wrapped around my thighs.

I groan out loud and blow out a breath while beads of sweat trickle down my back. Never in my life have I come this many times or this hard. Not that I had much experience. Chris never really tried beyond maybe once or twice. He always just fucked and came whenever he wanted, and that was that. I didn't mind … I could rub one out later when he was asleep.

But now, I have no choice in the matter. No way to stop it all.

If only Chris was here, maybe he'd free me from this mess.

The buzzing continues, harder and harder, and my body quakes like never before. My lungs fill with oxygen as I'm trying to breathe through this sexual energy raging through my body, ravaging all the modesty I had left. When the peak nears, I scream, and I fall apart once again, my eyes almost rolling into the back of my head.

My body falls forward as I hang in the cuffs, willing to give up anything and everything if it meant that this would stop. I would say yes to it all.

I peer through my half-closed eyes as the door cracks open, my body so wasted that I can't tell if someone is really there or not. The sound of a door closing pulls me back into the here and now, and my eyes burst open.

Eli walks closer, and I instinctively inch back against the wall, but I'm too exhausted to fight. He sits down on the bed beside me. I'd expected him to be ravenous, arrogant, enraged at my will to fight. But the gentleness in his eyes confuses the fuck out of me.

"How many times did you come?" he asks.

"Too many times …" I mutter.

"Have you had enough?"

I nod because I'm too drowsy to speak.

He smiles. "Are you ready to do anything and everything I demand from you?"

My lips part, and my face scrunches up as I try to form the words I so desperately want to speak, but I know it's a betrayal to my own morals if I do. But what choice do I have when faced with more of this?

"Yes," I murmur.

I didn't know I was that easy, that willing to give in. I guess that's what constant orgasms will do to one's resolve.

"Ask," he says.

"Please … can the buzzing stop?" I beg. "I'll do anything."

A devilish smile spreads on his lips. "Good little angel," he says, and he crawls on top of the bed and leans over me. "Because this will be much easier to you if you just give in."

When he unlatches the cuffs around my wrist, I simply cease to care and let my hands fall down to my sides.

His hand dives into his pocket, and he presses a button. The buzzing stops, and sweet, heavenly bliss follows. My entire pussy feels numb, and my clit is still swollen and raw from all the times I came. But with the buzzing gone, my entire body shakes uncontrollably and tears well up in my eyes.

Eli pulls me into him, wrapping his arms around me as though he wants to hug me. And for some reason, I don't want to fight it anymore. Instead, I yield into his warm embrace and let the devil comfort me, no matter how evil it is. Tears flow freely as he gently caresses my back, reminding me of what it feels like to be touched by someone. I can't remember the last time my boyfriend ever touched me like this, so warm and kindly as though there isn't anything I could do wrong. And it moves me to the point of wanting to hug him back.

But this is my captor. The man who just plucked me out of the library and shoved me into his car. I shouldn't feel any of these things when I'm around him, and the fact I do makes it even more confusing.

"That's it, angel … let it all out," he says, caressing me like I'm his pet.

And I don't even mind. I'll take this over that buzzing between my legs any day. In fact, it feels so good that my whole body just relaxes in his arms, like I've waited for his embrace since he came into my room. And now my emotions are a whirlwind of a mess.

He picks me up and carries me in his arms all the way to the private bathroom. There he sets me down on the chair and turns on the faucet in the bathtub. He goes to his knees and takes off my heels that I couldn't kick off in bed because of the straps. He softly places them on the floor beside me while his hand creeps up my leg ever so gently like a lover would touch his woman. And I'm so terribly confused by my own body's reaction to his petting that I just go along with it.

His hands slide all the way up my dress, creeping underneath the fabric, only to tug at the panties that hold the buzzer in place. My thighs unclench, and he slowly tugs the panties down my legs so carefully that I'm almost starting to wonder if he won't dare to touch me.

But that makes no sense. He captured me like a goddamn animal and keeps me in a cage. Why would he go through all that trouble if he could just grab what he wanted and use me?

I shiver in place from just the thought. And he pauses with undressing me right as the panties are at my toes.

"Don't think so much, Amelia," he says. "It will make you lose your mind."

"Too late," I respond, trying not to look at him, but it's so damn hard when he looks at me like that, so warm yet so possessive, like a teacher trying to woo his assistant into submission.

Before I can say another word, he slips my dress over my head and takes it off. When he sets his eyes on me, I clench my legs together and clutch my chest.

"Why do you want to hide so badly?" he asks.

I throw him a look and don't respond, but he knows

damn well why.

He shrugs and turns around, feeling the temperature of the water before flicking his hand to rid himself of the droplets. "It's warm enough. Hop in."

I lift a brow and look at him. "Why?"

"You're dirty," he retorts, cocking his head. "Didn't you feel the beads of sweat dripping down your back while you were coming?"

I almost choke on my own saliva. I can't believe he said that out loud. And for some reason, it makes my cheeks flush with heat.

He nods at the water. "Go on."

I hesitate for a moment, staring at him just to gauge how pissed off he'd get if I didn't do what he says. Maybe now wouldn't be the smartest time to do that. I mean, he's warming up to me, and it'd be a shame to waste his trust. Maybe I can use it to my advantage. If I make him believe I'm a good girl … would it be easier to fool him until I find a way out?

I gather my courage and get up from the seat, still clutching myself as I huddle toward the bathtub and step inside. The water is warm and feels so good on my aching body, but I can't enjoy it because he's still here staring at me.

"What do you want me to do?" I ask.

"Clean yourself," he answers.

Waiting, I continue to stare at him, hoping he'll leave, but he doesn't.

"What are you waiting for?" he asks.

"Can I have a little privacy?"

He shakes his head and grabs another strand of my hair, twirling it in his fingers. "Perhaps. But you'll have to earn my trust, angel."

Goose bumps scatter on my skin. I lean away so my hair falls from his fingers. "Fine. Can I at least have a towel or something? To cover up?"

He leans in over the bathtub, taking in a deep breath while he momentarily closes his eyes, almost as if he's savoring the smell. "There is nothing to hide, Amelia. I've already seen enough … and I enjoyed every second of it."

My cheeks turn crimson red. When he opens his eyes again, we engage in a stare down, and my whole body begins to shake again.

"You get off on this, don't you?" I retort.

A smirk spreads on his lips. "Not enough."

I throw him a shady look. "I'd like to know what kind of evil deserves this punishment," I growl, rage bubbling up to the surface again.

"That's something you need to find out for yourself," he says.

I roll my eyes and throw my head back, groaning with annoyance.

He grips my hand. "You begged me to, Amelia. Do not forget."

"But if I ask you to let me go, you'll refuse, won't you?"

"Because that's not what you need," he retorts.

Tears well up in my eyes again. "I just want my freedom

back … please."

I'm hoping, praying, that my pleading will have an effect on him, but he doesn't seem the least bit fazed. It's almost as if he's seen me do this a million times before. Like he's grown used to it. And that makes me wonder … am I the first girl he's done this to?

"Your freedom is tied to your punishment …"

I rub my lips together and look away. "Right."

"All you have to do is confess and forgive."

Confess and forgive?

I make a tsk sound. As if it's so easy. Like I can just call out whatever I did and end this. Like I can just forgive him after all this.

"How can I forgive *you*?" I ask.

"It's not *me* who needs forgiving," he replies, raising his brow at me when I turn my head to face him.

My pupils dilate as the realization of what he means hits me.

"I know you think it's impossible, but give it time," he says.

"You want to keep me here in this gilded cage, but you won't tell me why, and all you wanna do is punish me because I asked?" My lip trembles. "What if I told you a lie? Huh? What if I never meant it? What if I just wanted attention?"

He glares right back at me as though he can see straight through me. And the palm of his hand rises to meet my face, caressing my cheek so softly that it almost makes me turn into putty. "A girl like you doesn't lie. She only forgets."

Then he gets up and walks out the door, but not before adding, "Clean yourself and put on a nightgown. My assistant will be watching you, so don't try anything."

Someone? Watching me? How?

Then it hits me.

There's a reason they knew exactly when to come into my room. And why he's so sure of the fact that I won't harm him, or that I could escape if I tried.

There are cameras.

ELEVEN

ELI

"How is she doing?"

I sit down in my chair and pick up my glass of whiskey, taking a sip before I answer Tobias's question.

"Fine," I reply.

For the situation she's in, anyway. But I'm not keen on divulging much. A part of me knows it would be beneficial if I did, but I don't trust him enough to explain every little detail of what went down. I know he's waiting for me to mess up, but I won't give him that satisfaction. Not willingly anyway.

"Fine how? Scared? In pain? Completely out of it?"

I clutch my chair and stare at him with intent as he keeps digging for more. "Does it matter? I'm handling it."

I'm doing this my way. Slow and gentle, so she gets eased into it. With a girl like her, that's definitely necessary.

It'll be hard but not impossible.

"Well, I need to know how our newest addition is doing," he says, clutching his hands together and leaning forward. "There's no way of telling how she'll react, and we need to be prepared."

"I don't need your lecture, Tobias. I know how it works." I put my glass down again.

His brow rises. "I'm just saying, maybe we should keep tabs."

"The cameras do their job just fine," I retort.

"I know that," he says, looking at me from underneath his lashes. "But are you sure you can control her?" He narrows his eyes at me, and I do the same in response. I know he's testing me, and I know damn well why. "Because it looks to me as though you can't control yourself either."

My fingers dig into the leather seat. "I'm fine. I've got this. Don't worry about it. Keep your eyes on your own job."

"I just don't want this to backfire." He leans forward in his seat. "You know we have a protocol. We don't pick up the girls. They are brought to us. Bringing them in like this out of the blue is really dangerous. Especially if they can't even remember—"

I slam my fist onto the elbow rest. "Enough!"

He sits back and cocks his head. "In control, you said? Do you even see your own wrath?"

He's just pushing me, but I won't let him test me like this.

I look at the fire instead of his eyes. "You do remember who leads this House, don't you?" With renewed energy, I gaze at him, determined not to let him poke at my boundaries. "What are you?"

"An advisor," he says, sighing.

"Exactly. So behave like it."

"I try," he says with another sigh. "But you won't let me."

"I don't need you to belittle my choices. I picked her up for a reason. She needs this," I reply.

"If you say so," he mutters, turning to gaze at the fire. "But she's volatile. She will fight this more than any other. And if she manages to escape, this whole place could be exposed."

"She won't," I say. I pick up my whiskey and take another sip. God only knows I need it. "I'll make sure of that."

***

Amelia

When my eyes open, it feels as though minutes have passed, but the sun is already blinding me.

Fuck.

I failed.

My muscles ache and my bones creak as I try to get up from the wooden chair. Oh God, I really shouldn't have fallen asleep here, out of all places.

Apparently, my body couldn't take another night of no sleep.

I groan and rub my eyes, wishing I could slap myself, but that would do me no good. I should've just stayed awake.

I even looked at myself in the mirror last night just to force myself to stay in the moment. My eyes were red and puffy, but the rest of me was as white as a ghost. But when I tried to sit down to take a moment of rest, I still slipped away even though I avoided the comfy bed with that soft blanket and heavenly pillow that I was dying to drown myself into.

And all I could think about at that moment was that man. Eli. And how he could make me beg with a simple stare. Just the memory of him strapping me to the bed makes goose bumps scatter on my skin again.

One minute, he was a gentleman, his touch like feathers on my skin, and the next, he trapped me on the bed and forced me to come over and over until I was completely wasted. Is that my punishment? Is this what I deserve?

No, I mustn't think like that. None of this is my fault. I didn't ask for any of this.

But you did ask him to punish you.

I close my eyes and force myself to remember why, but

I can't for the life of me bring it to the forefront of my mind. All I remember is the guilt swirling through my veins with every step I took, every book I placed back in the bookcase, every word I uttered.

I am guilty. And I need to be punished.

But for what?

I groan to myself, wishing I wasn't such a mystery, even to myself.

But Eli knows … he knows exactly what I did, and he won't tell me. Not until I've succumbed to every one of his devilish, twisted ideas.

What else does he have in store for me?

I rub the bridge of my nose. I wish I could remember why I'd even say those damn words, but the longer I mull over it, the more I'm coming up with blanks.

Maybe I only said it because I was bored with my life, and when I was trapped by this handsome stranger offering a chance at something else, I took it. And that's exactly why he did it. Why he pretended to be so charming, why he was such a gentleman to begin with …. To lure me in.

My hand balls into a fist, and I slam it onto the elbow rest. "Dammit!"

I'm just making myself crazy by rehashing it all. I'm still stuck here in this room that's more like a gilded prison than anything else. There are only two ways out of here—one is by force, and the other is by playing along until I can find a way to escape.

And I've already deduced option one isn't worth the

risk. I was never a fighter anyway … but I am a thinker, so surely, this brain can find a way out of this mess I started, can't it?

Suddenly, the door handle is pushed down, and I jolt up from the chair and bolt to the corner of the room, one of only two spots not seen by the cameras. Yeah, I've done my research. Last night I looked at all of the ones I could find and pinpointed their reach by watching them move. Lucky for me, there are blind spots where I'll be at least a little bit safer. As far as safety is ever possible in a house like this.

Who knows what lies beyond those doors that just opened. I don't.

But she does.

Her footsteps are like light little taps as the girl steps inside. The door is still open behind her, and I marvel at it as though it's a gateway into another world.

"Eli requests that you have breakfast with him." She adds a gentle smile. "But you need to get dressed first."

I look at my feet and back up again at the flimsy nightgown I'm wearing. I'd completely forgotten that I'd put this on. After he bathed me, I kind of zoned out, but just looking at myself makes everything flood back into my mind. How he came into my room after I'd been coming for hours on end and unlocked me when I begged him to. How he picked me up and carried me to the bathroom, then stripped me naked and put me in the tub. How warm and nice the water felt on my aching skin. And how gentle he was with me.

I shrug it off and force myself to stop thinking about him that way. A man like him, who just whisks someone out of their comfort zone and into captivity, cannot be kind.

The girl walks to the wardrobe and opens it up, rummaging through the clothes before saying, "Aha!"

Holding out a white dress with frills above my shoulder, she narrows her eyes and thins her lips as though she's thinking hard. "No. Never mind." She goes back to the wardrobe and sticks her head inside while I just stand there watching her.

Again, she pulls out a dress. This time, it's a little black dress with studded gems on the rims of the shoulder straps. She holds it over my body and smiles gleefully. "Perfect."

I frown. "Is this really necessary?"

She cocks her head and furrows her brows right back at me. "Of course, silly. You need to look perfect for Eli."

She bends over, pulls my nightgown straight over my head, and throws it aside.

I cover my boobs while she picks up the new dress. "Here. Put it on."

"Why do you do all of this?" I ask, trying to reason with her in the hopes of gaining a new ally even though her frivolousness makes me want to scream. "Don't you see he's keeping me a prisoner here?"

"Everyone says that," she says, shrugging. "No one knows how badly they need this until it's all over."

I make a face. "Who is everyone?" I ask, my heart racing in my chest. "There are *others*?"

She sucks in a breath until her chest grows tight and her lips are thin. "I'm not in a position to discuss those matters," she says. "But rest assured that Eli only wants the best for you."

She throws the new dress over my head and pulls it down my legs. "There. Go on, have a look." She nudges me toward the mirror. "Beautiful, right?"

I look at myself, but all I see is a vapid shell of a girl.

But I don't know if that's because I was brought here … or because of what came before.

"Why do you help him?" I ask, staring at her through the mirror, wondering why any girl would ever do this to another.

She places her hands on my shoulders and rubs her lips together. "Because I've seen what he can do, and I believe in it wholeheartedly."

I turn around to face her. "What does he do? You have to tell me why he did this to me."

She sighs and shakes her head. "I'm sorry, I can't. It's not my place."

"But you must know, right?"

She shakes her head again. "Sorry. I don't know about your sins. Like I said, I simply do the chores and help where help is needed."

My stomach churns, and I look down at my feet. "Okay."

This girl probably won't be of much use after all. So much for getting allies.

"Oh, right! I forgot!" Her cheerfulness has me momentarily lift my head in the hopes that it's worth it. But when she pulls a pair of pumps from the wardrobe, my heart immediately sinks into my shoeless feet.

She goes to her knees and puts on the pair of pumps like I'm Cinderella waiting to be picked up by Prince Charming. But Eli is no Prince, and nothing about being kept like a prisoner is charming.

She puts up this huge smile when she's done. "You look gorgeous. Ready?"

I shake my head. "No."

She laughs. "Of course you are, silly." She winks. "Unless you mean you still need to put on your special panties."

My eyes widen. Special panties. Does she mean …?

"No," I blurt out.

"Relax, I'm just kidding." She taps my shoulder, and it's the first time in ages I've had the urge to bite someone's fingers off. "If Eli wanted you to wear something underneath your dress, you'd know."

So I'm going naked? I shiver from the thought. From all the things I'm imagining right now, all the ways Eli might touch me underneath the table, his calloused hands sliding across my thigh.

I clench my legs together.

Can I even do this? Can I play along without losing myself in this game of his?

The girl turns around and beckons me. "C'mon. He's

waiting."

"Wait," I say as she opens the door again. She pauses, so I ask, "What's your name?"

"Mary," she replies.

"I'm Amelia," I say. "Nice to meet you."

I don't want to be nice, and nothing about this is nice, but I don't want to burn my bridges just yet. Maybe she could be of some use, someday.

She snorts. "Eli already told me your name."

Right. Of course, he has. Nothing is secret here in this *House of Sin.*

She promptly spins on her heels again, her movements featherlight like a bird fluttering off.

I swallow and push myself away from the wall again. I could stay, fight against the command to have breakfast with him, but what good would that do me? Just so he can come and give me more punishment?

The mere thought of being pinned to that bed and forced to come again makes me quiver. It's better for me if I just do what he wants for now.

So I sigh and walk toward the light that shines brightly behind the doors. Adrenaline shoots through my veins as I open the door farther and step outside into what feels like purgatory itself.

But the second I look up, my jaw drops. I'm on the first floor of a giant hallway with an overlooking balcony covered in flowers. The entire thing is made out of stone, like an ancient castle. Red carpets line the hallway, and seats and statues are placed along the way between each room. All rooms have numbers, and when I gaze over my shoulder, I notice one on mine too: Twenty-six.

I look back around and stop to momentarily gaze over the edge of the balcony. The room below is huge, maybe as big as an entire theater, and there is one broad wooden staircase in the middle, with two smaller circular staircases at each side, leading all the way up to the second floor. Paintings cover the ceiling, and a giant circle in the middle consists entirely of window panels, allowing the light to fill the area.

Never in my life have I seen such opulence. Then again, it's not like I went out a lot, especially not with people as rich as Eli must be. Unless … this isn't just his house but someone else's too.

I gulp at the thought and push it away as we make our way to the staircase.

There are so many rooms here that it makes me wonder what's in each of them. How many people live here? Or is this all just one man's ultimate fantasy come to life?

When I was still at the library, some of those books near the romance fiction aisle would sometimes mention houses like this, but never in my wildest dreams would I have thought I'd end up in one myself. Nor in the position that I currently find myself in.

As we approach the stairs, the girl suddenly stops at the top.

"Mary."

His voice makes my heart stop.

"You can leave the rest to me now."

I stop walking and watch the girl bow out. She signals me with just her eyes to come to the top of the stairs. My legs are shaking, my body feeling heavier with every step I take. When I turn and look, he's right there at the bottom of the stairs, waiting for me.

A soft smile forms on his lips, one that tugs at my heartstrings. "You look … beautiful."

Beautiful … a compliment that would bring the flush to my cheeks, even when this black dress is just another prison strapped around my body.

A prison he put there just to enjoy himself.

I don't smile back.

"C'mon." He holds out his hand, and we engage in a stare off for a moment before I finally cave and take the steps downstairs, each one of them making my heart pound even harder.

I reach out; even though my heart tells me not to, my brain knows this is the smarter choice. When our hands touch, it's as if lightning shoots through my veins, and it reminds me of the first time we met. When he was still only a handsome stranger I wished would sweep me off my feet.

How poetic, these fantasies of mine.

"Thank you for coming," he says, and he lifts my hand to his mouth again and presses another kiss to it, almost making me forget what kind of a man he really is. If he is a man at all because underneath this chiseled, rugged face and black-suited façade hides a beast.

Before releasing my hand, he looks up at me from underneath his dark lashes and says, "Did you sleep well?"

My lips twitch. This is a test, isn't it? It has to be. Someone like him wouldn't ask a question like this without it having some ulterior motive attached. Because this question's followed by the most smoldering of stares.

"I … Uh …" I mutter. "Yes."

A dirty smile creeps up onto his lips. "Is that the truth?"

My eyes widen, and I feel caught in the act. The truth … he mentioned wanting that before. But this isn't the truth he was looking for.

He leans in and whispers into my ear, "Do not lie to me, Amelia."

And I can't fucking breathe.

"I …"

"It's okay," he says, and he leans away again, just a little. Not far enough to create space, but far enough to look me in the eyes and caress my cheek. "You will learn that it comes with a price."

My pupils dilate, and my lungs contract. Only when he moves back can I breathe once again.

Should I say sorry? No, that probably wouldn't matter to him. He isn't the type to accept takebacks. I've learned that much in my short time of being here.

"Now, let's eat," he says, a dirty smile on his face. "I'm sure you're famished."

I nod and swallow, and he releases my hand. It suddenly

feels cold and bare. He turns around and walks off, and I follow him, unsure what else I should or can do. A part of me wants to run and hide, but an assistant or guard is standing by at every corner.

Do they all work for Eli? And is this Eli's home? Or is there more to this than I can see with my own naked eyes?

I notice Eli has already gone up ahead into the dining room, so I stop gaping around and rush to the door, terrified of more consequences. But the minute I step inside, I pause, and my lungs constrict to the point of making it impossible to breathe.

There he is, situated at the head of the table, two men right beside him, both looking at me as if I'm the star of the show.

We're not alone.

TWELVE

Amelia

Three men sit upon their throne, gazing up at me as though they own this room and everything in it … including me. But they sit on a throne of lies.

Who are these men? Eli never told me there were more involved. How far do his schemes go, and what do they plan on doing with me?

Eli beckons me. "Come."

I take a deep breath and step forward, every step I make reverberating against the tiled floors to the same rhythm as my thrumming heart. Each step is another one closer into the clutches of these men. But there is no turning around, no going back.

This beautiful house is my prison now, whether I like it

or not, and I have no choice but to play their game and hope I get out unscathed. But at what cost?

"Sit," Eli says, but he doesn't point at any chair, and there are many.

Which one do I pick? Is this a trick? A game I need to win?

My mind can't stop thinking of all the possible options, all the things that he could do to me if I pick the wrong one, and for some reason, a flash of excitement flushes through me.

I swallow hard as the three men look at me while I approach one of the chairs.

One of them has a laid-back look on his scruffy face with his dark brown hair cut short at the top, but a darkness hides in those pristine blue eyes. The other guy at the table looks away as though he's annoyed by my mere presence. With that blond beard and undercut ponytail, he looks like a goddamn Viking. But that might just be my imagination running away with me.

Eli taps his fingers on the table, clearly impatient, and I grab the chair and scoot it back. It's farthest away from them all, on the side of the guy with the long hair. I figured I had better chances of not being gaped at by sitting here, but I'm not sure it's doing me any good. Eli's watchful gaze is still upon me, and now I'm starting to wonder if I picked the right chair.

"Interesting," he murmurs. "You chose a seat farthest away from the three of us." He adds a possessive smile, one that reminds me of that time he came into my room and plucked me off the bed and peeled away my clothes to put me in the tub, one that makes goose bumps scatter on my skin.

The guy with the blue eyes sighs. "Eli, enough with the games."

Eli lifts his finger, and the guy promptly shuts his mouth. Eli must be the one in charge then.

I don't respond. Not even as the stares and silence get awkward.

"We should introduce ourselves." He glances over at the men at his right-hand side and then his left. "Go on."

The blue-eyed guy raises his brows at me. "Name's Tobias."

"And who are you?" I ask, raising a brow too.

He sports a smile. "I am Eli's advisor."

I lean back in my chair and fold my arms. "Advisor to what, exactly? Eli's little games?"

His tongue briefly darts out to wet his lips. "I see you've already been acquainted."

"So you know what he did to me, right?" I ask, full-on staring at him now. "That he stole me right out of the library and locked me up in here like I'm some kind of prisoner?"

Tobias doesn't reply. He just stares right back at me, so I roll my eyes and sigh. "Thought so."

Eli clears his throat and nods at the blond-haired guy. "That's Soren."

"He can't tell me himself?" I ask.

Eli blinks slowly. "He speaks only when needed."

"Why is that?" I ask.

Eli narrows his eyes at me, and the whole room suddenly feels tense as hell.

Did I overstep?

"Enough questions. Let's just start with breakfast, shall we?" Tobias says.

"Right. Where are my manners?" Eli muses.

He claps his hands, and out pour waiters with plates of food that smell delicious and make my mouth water. Each plate is filled with copious amounts of fruit, various types of bread, some butter, a glass of milk and coffee, as well as some eggs and a few strips of bacon. It's more than I could possibly eat even though I'm famished.

Is this a test too? Are they waiting for me to make a choice? To eat or grab a knife and throw it at them? Or maybe the food is poisoned.

Panic rushes through my veins. They wouldn't, right? Or maybe he would … after all, Eli did say I did something bad and that I deserved to be punished. Maybe death is a part of the punishment.

I'm not so hungry anymore.

"Amelia …" Eli muses. "Aren't you going to eat?"

Even his accomplices, Tobias and Soren, are eating to their heart's content. The first with elegance and manners, the second as though he's devouring a spit roast at an eating competition.

I turn my gaze at all the delicious food lying on my plate

and bite my lip, wishing I could take a bite, wishing I knew if it would kill me or not. But I don't want to take that chance. My life is still worth living.

At least … as long as I manage to get out of this mess. Because who knows how long these men will keep me here.

Eli cocks his head when I don't respond. "You are hungry, though, right?"

I throw him a deadly stare.

He looks at me as though I've lost my mind. "It's food, Amelia. You don't trust us, do you?"

"No," I reply shortly. Tobias snorts, which makes Eli throw him a look to shut him up.

Soren hasn't even spoken to me since I came here, and I don't think he'll jump in any time soon either.

Eli gazes at me again with blazing fury in his eyes. "It is not poisoned, if that's what you think."

Maybe. Maybe not. Who knows. I can't trust a thing he says. So I shove the plate away so I don't have to smell all that good stuff.

"Fine. You don't want to eat? Then don't," he retorts, his voice in stark contrast with before. He picks up his fork and starts slicing his bacon into bits. "I gave you a choice."

"What … is that supposed to mean?" I almost choke on my own words.

He stops slicing for a moment. "It means that you have a choice. In everything. And that choice determines the next actions."

"Next actions?" I hold my breath.

He can't mean …

He looks up at me with devilish eyes. "Every choice has a consequence, angel."

Tears well up in my eyes, and in a bout of rage I throw my napkin out onto the table. "I didn't ask for any of this!"

"Yes, you did," he replies stoically as though it doesn't affect him to see me in pain like this.

The other men are silently complicit in his trickery.

"If I'd known, I would've never said those words," I growl.

He takes a bite of his bacon and swallows it down before replying. "But you did, and now look where we are."

"You made this choice, not me," I say, shaking my head.

"This is all on you, angel," he says, leaning back in his chair. "Look, we can talk about it all day long, but nothing will change. You will still be here, in my domain … my house, doing exactly. What. I. Say." He pronounces each syllable separately as if to add more weight to the already heavy words. "And it is about time you started to respect that."

I grind my teeth and refuse to respond.

"Now eat. This is your last chance."

I stare at the plate in front of me, wondering what will happen if I don't do what he asks. Before I came downstairs, I told myself I'd comply, but that was before I learned more men were keeping me here. More secrets, more lies. Even if I played along, who knows what else he keeps hidden from me. What else he could use to keep me here.

Even though I hate conflict with all my guts, I cannot in good conscience do as he wishes. But what will it cost me? And am I willing to throw it all away just over a bit of food?

I gulp, considering my options.

All three men are busy eating their food, but not me. I can't stop staring at it, like it's a ticking time bomb. *Tick. Tick. Tick.* A clock on the wall behind me adds to the pressure. Soon there won't be any more time left to make the decision.

Eat or don't eat. That's the choice. But I can't make it, no matter how hard I try. I scoot closer, pick up my fork and pull the plate closer. But one look at that gleeful face makes me stop in my tracks again.

This is what he wants. He wants me to give in and let him control me. To admit I was wrong and he was right all along … that I need to be punished … that I deserve whatever I have coming for me.

No way.

I shove it back even harder than before, throw my cutlery onto the table, and scoot my chair back, standing up in defiance against my captors.

"No." I say it with such certainty that I almost have myself fooled.

My heartbeat rapidly increases at the sight of his eyes that flash with rage. It can only mean one thing … punishment.

ELI

All the forks and knives are placed down on the table.

What is she doing? Is she trying to … defy me?

A smile tugs at my lips. Well … I never imagined she'd have this much spunk left in her after what I did. But maybe I shouldn't be so surprised either, considering I picked her.

"Shouldn't have done that, angel," I murmur.

I raise my hand, and her eyes follow. As my fingers snap, her pupils dilate, and two of my men appear from the sidelines to take her away.

She doesn't squeal, doesn't kick, doesn't even fight them off. Like a true queen, she accepts her defeat and walks with them, as though she knew this was the only outcome to her defiance. With grace, she allows them to escort her out of the room, but right before she exits, she still throws one last glance over her shoulder.

Not at the food, though I'm sure she's more than hungry and wishing she would've stayed. No, the stare is directly pointed at me, as a sort of threat. As if she means to say … I might give in now, but I'm not going to yield to you.

But we both know I will never stop until she does.

And when that time comes, I will savor it most of all.

THIRTEEN

Amelia

A hundred and thirty hours.

I counted each minute.

Not at the beginning … when it was still easy, and I still had energy left to entertain myself in other ways, like by reading one of the many books from the bookshelf on the wall or cleaning the room I was forced to inhabit anyway. But slowly, my vision started blurring with each letter I tried to read, and my body was quaking every time I tried to scrub the sink with a cloth from the stack. And eventually, I could only lie in bed and wait.

And wait I have … every minute spent counting the time.

Next to the locked door, that clock hanging on my wall,

ticking away, is my biggest enemy right now. It forces me to come face-to-face with my new reality: That I am stuck here and don't know for how long.

A hundred and thirty hours ... that's how long I've been here since I told Eli "no."

I didn't know then what it would mean.

What I would be giving up.

That it would force me not to only admit that I am not free to do what I want, say what I want ... but also that each of my actions have consequences.

Instead of eating that scrumptious food, I chose to deny him just because of fear and pride.

It's the last time I saw food.

Any kind, whatsoever.

I've been drinking water from the tap from a glass ever since. Just a few gulps at first to quench my thirst, but as the days passed, I started replacing the emptiness in my stomach with water. At least it would calm my hunger for a little while to make me forget.

But every passing day has made me shakier, more tired, more ... everything.

The more I force myself to think of something else, the less it works. Food is all I can think about even though I know I'll survive. At least, for now. A human body is capable of so much. But I never imagined the mental toll it takes, and that, more than anything, is the real struggle.

With every passing second, I grow more lethargic and complacent.

Soon, my resolve will crumble.

I will beg.

I will plead.

Even if the food is poisoned, I would probably eat it with glee, knowing it was my last meal … at least I'd die with a full stomach.

I can't think like that, but being hungry does that to a person's mind.

Maybe this is my real punishment. Not the lack of food but the breakdown of all the resolve and dignity that comes with it.

Groaning, I roll over in bed, but my growling stomach won't stop waking me up. I can't fucking sleep, not when I lie down nor when I sit up, and it's maddening.

All I can think of is slamming my fists onto that door and begging.

Beg for them to let me out.

Tell them I'm willing to do anything …

But what would that make of me?

Would I be a coward for giving in?

All of it, the defiance, staying here without food, the buzzing panties … will all have been for nothing.

But I can't take it anymore.

With the last bit of energy I have left, I throw the blanket off and set my feet on the floor. I groan and force myself to ignore the looming headache as I get up and walk to the door. I reach for the wood with a shaky hand and pound on it a few times.

"I give up," I murmur.

There's no response. No sound. Nothing.

Nothing to suggest anyone's there.

"Please … I take it back," I murmur. "I want to eat."

I know he doesn't do takebacks, and once I've said something, it's taken seriously. Which is why I hope he's capable of growth too. I have to pray he doesn't just keep me here for the sake of punishing me … just to let me die.

No, he wants to keep me alive, so I'm sure this will work. Right?

I turn my head and gaze at the cameras I've found. I know he's watching me. He must know what I said. What I begged for.

So why is it taking so long?

I plant my forehead against the door and breathe out a few sighs. Was it all worth it? I said I wouldn't eat, that I didn't trust them, but what difference did it make? Sitting here in my room doing nothing while I could've tried my best to manipulate him and get out …

"You won. I lost," I mutter against the wood.

And I sink to the floor with my back against the door, huddling my legs close to me.

After a few minutes, the door handle is pushed down.

I quickly crawl away and scramble to gather myself while still on the floor as the door creaks open and in steps a foot.

I expected Mary to come and get me so I could eat downstairs again.

But it's Eli himself wearing merely a button-down white

shirt and a pair of black pants coupled with a big shiny gold belt buckle, and in his hands, he has a big plate filled with food, the mere smell making my mouth water.

But when my eyes rise to meet his, they almost burn a hole into me. I gulp and settle down on the floor, realizing that none of this will come easy.

Food is never really just food.

It's a bargaining chip.

And he wants … submission.

***

ELI

Her fragile, small body sits on the carpeted floor, her eyes full of hunger but also something else. Betrayal.

A smirk forms on my lips as I step farther inside and close the door behind me, the clicking of the lock the only sound in this room.

She stays put in the middle as though she's frozen in time, only the rise and fall of her shoulders with every shallow breath giving life away.

I lick my lips and tip the plate forward, allowing her to see what's on top. She momentarily glances at the food, her tongue darting out to wet her lips at the sight of the sweet pancakes with whipped cream and strawberries on top. A personal favorite of mine, especially for moments such as these.

Her body leans in, almost as if it's lured forward on its own by the promise of food. But her brain kicks in and forces her to stop, her fingers digging into the skin of her thighs.

It is a beautiful thing to watch the mind unravel and be overtaken by the body.

And we haven't even started yet.

I place the plate down on the cabinet next to the door, and her eyes immediately home in on it as though she's contemplating snatching it right out from underneath my nose. But she's not the first who has attempted that, and I don't think I have to remind her she won't be successful because the very next thing she does is eyeball me to gauge my reaction.

I'm not easily persuaded to give in.

And she knows this too.

"Why did you come?" she asks.

I point at the camera in the corner. "You knew those were there ... that's why you looked."

She swallows as the muscles in her body grow tenser. "So you did hear me." She glares at the food again, almost as if she's mad that I brought it up here.

My brow rises, and I lean against the cabinet, blocking her view of the food. "Someone always keeps an eye on you."

"Great ..." She sighs and folds her arms. "And

126

perverted."

I snort and smile at her comment. "Not when you go to the toilet."

She narrows her eyes. "That doesn't make it any better."

I cock my head and shrug. "I think so, personally."

"Are you just here to chitchat with me?" she asks.

I release the cabinet and take a step toward her. She immediately jumps up to her feet and steps away. When I stop, she sinks to the floor again as though she regrets ever moving.

"I came … because you begged," I answer.

Her eyes bore into mine. Another swallow.

I loosen my cuffs and slide them up to my elbows, capturing her attention with a simple show of dominance. I grab the plate from the cabinet again and walk toward her, holding it tightly in my hand so she won't be able to steal something.

Towering over her, I look down at her from underneath my lashes. "Kneel."

She frowns for a second, then looks confused, her eyes constantly wandering off to the plate. Her mouth must be watering at the sight. But there is a price to pay for defiance. A sin is followed by punishment.

"Is that what you want?"

When I don't reply, she changes positions, swiftly spinning around so her legs are no longer in front of her but behind her, and her ass lowers onto her heels.

Good. Finally, she obeys.

I step closer and look at the beauty in front of me, at the woman below me who is dying for this meal ... who would be willing to give her freedom, and all that it entails, away for a simple bite.

I go on one knee, still clutching the plate tightly, and reach for the fork.

When she does the same, I pull away again.

She stops and eyes me. "I thought I could eat."

"You can ..." I say. "On *my* terms."

A scowl forms on her face. "That's not fair."

I raise a brow. "You asked for this, remember?"

"I asked for food," she retorts.

"And *you* asked to be punished."

Her lips part, but she doesn't reply, so I take that as an acknowledgment.

"You begged me for food ... now let me give you what you need," I say as I lean in.

She makes a face at me. "Why can't I just feed myself?"

I don't answer because she knows why.

I am the captor; she is the captive. I am the one who punishes; she is the one who sins. There is no other way around, no reasoning, no bargaining to be done. This is it. This is the deal she made.

"How many more rules are there?" she asks.

"As many as I see fit," I answer, and I grab the fork and stick on some of the pre-cut pancakes. "Now ..." I swirl the fork through the whipped cream. "Open up."

When the fork approaches her mouth, she still refuses

to yield.

"It is not poisoned," I offer as a sign of good faith.

"How do I know for sure?" she asks, her eyes flickering with uncertainty.

A smile forms on my lips. So mistrustful. "You don't."

"But I—"

"But *you begged*," I interrupt, throwing her a look.

She shuts her mouth again and gazes at me with both rage and fear swirling in her eyes. Rage at me coming in here to feed her like she's a child and fear for not knowing what more I could demand if she surrenders.

And that's what she needs to understand. There is no choice. No ifs, ands, or buts.

"Do as I say, and you will be all right," I say.

"Will I be free?" she asks, lowering her eyes to the carpet. "If I eat this food, will you let me go?"

I force her chin up. "Only you have that power …"

"I don't understand what you mean. I don't have any power here."

I peer into her eyes. "Freedom comes at a price, a price you're not willing to pay … yet."

She turns her head away as I approach with the fork again, the aroma luring her nostrils to turn her head again so she can see just how delicious these pancakes are.

My face softens for a moment, and I lean in to tilt her chin up again. "This is what *you* want. Now eat."

Finally, her lips part, and her mouth opens. I slide the fork onto her tongue, taking ample time to enjoy the sheer pleasure of an obedient angel chewing on and swallowing the food I have given her.

"Good girl," I murmur.

I pick up a strawberry and run it through the whipped cream. Her eyes follow my every move as though she's wondering what I'm going to do ... what else I *could* do with these fingers of mine.

Oh, there is plenty ... but I will take it slowly with her. I'll wait and coax her into doing exactly as I please. And we'll start with food.

I bring the strawberry up to her lips, circling them with the whipped cream until she opens them, never taking my eyes off her. I want her to know I'm watching and that I'm enjoying every second of dominating her.

And when her lips part and I push the strawberry inside, I simply can't stop the devilish grin from appearing on my face. Her cheeks flush with heat, and she quickly swallows the strawberry, almost afraid of the effect she has on me. But I don't mind ... at all.

With every bite and every swallow, my cock hardens against my pants. And as she takes more and more bites, my mind trails off to all the sinful things I wish to do to her, all the ways I could make her body yield to me ... about how good it would feel to have her tongue wrapped around my cock.

I groan with delight as she swallows, and she momentarily stops eating as I smile.

"Go on ... you were hungry, right?" I tip the fork

against her lips again, but her eyes trail off down my chest to my pants tenting from my stiff cock.

She gulps, her cheeks getting an even brighter shade of red, and it brings me such pleasure watching her crumble to desire.

She'd never admit out loud that she secretly wants me. But I'm sure she's considered it a few times, and the mere thought makes me want to pounce on her like a lion who's finally caught its prey.

But as long as she doesn't submit, she remains off-limits. Untouchable. Because it's not me who begged to be punished, it was her choice. And it should be her undoing.

I skewer the rest of the pancakes onto the fork and push them into her mouth until she swallows it all. A small smile appears and vanishes within a split second, but I caught it, and it makes my inner lion grumble with pleasure.

"You finished your plate," I muse.

She licks her lips and peeks over my shoulder as though she's wondering if there's more.

"Are you still hungry?" I ask.

She makes a face and looks away, her hands clenched on her knees.

I grab her chin and make her look at me. "You can have food as long as you obey the rules. Do you understand?"

She nods.

"When Mary tells you to come downstairs to eat with us, you will do so."

She doesn't reply, but I know she heard me.

"When I tell you to do *anything* … you will do exactly that."

"Why?" she asks. "If that's all a part of my punishment …" She licks her lips again and briefly glances down at my clearly tented pants. "What else is?"

My eyes flash with the same hunger hers showed mere minutes ago. "Everything."

FOURTEEN

Amelia

He gets up from the floor and places the plate of pancakes onto the cabinet, then sits down on the chair against the wall, his legs wide open. His fingers tap against each other as he stares at me with a daring look in his eyes as though I'm supposed to know what to do.

With renewed energy, I get up from the floor, my nightgown barely covering my private parts. I stand there staring right back at him.

"Come here," he says with an assertive voice.

I swallow back the lump in my throat. I can choose to fight him, to run and risk my chances. But the possibility of ending up having to endure countless hours without food or those orgasmic waves for hours on end is enough to make me want to forget that option even exists. Choosing to obey would be the easier choice ... but at what cost? My sanity.

Giving in to him means admitting that I need to submit. That he is right, and I am wrong. He's giving me the idea of a choice, but not the freedom that comes with it.

My legs are still shaky as I approach him, my stomach still growling as though it's trying to make up for all the lost food by eating it all in one go.

He beckons me as if to say, "There's more where that came from." All I need to do is beg.

Beg ... and obey. It all seems so simple, yet I cannot stop fighting the turmoil in my head.

He looks up at me from his seated position, taunting me to act. He has no weapon, nothing to keep me in place or stop me from attacking him. It's a test. I can sense it.

His eyes narrow. "Kneel."

I shudder but still do as he asks, realizing that doing so would be the safest choice. I bend through the knees until I'm on the floor in front of him. He cocks his head and leans over to grab a strand of my hair, only to slowly tuck it behind my ear. The gentleness of his touch catches me off guard.

How can a captor be so gentle and such a monster at the same time? Every single touch he gives me right now is one I crave, and I don't know why. Have I lost my mind already?

His thumb lingers near my mouth, a simple touch to my lips sending electricity down my spine. His finger still smells of strawberry pancakes and delicious sin. Mere minutes ago, he was feeding me with these same fingers. A man who denied me food and then gave it to me anyway just because I asked …

Confusion settles in slowly but surely, and judging from the haunting look on his face, that's exactly what he had planned.

He leans back again in the chair and places both hands on the armrests like a king judging his people. "Tell me again what you told me in that library," he says. "Your deepest, darkest wish."

I gasp. I've tried so hard not to remember why I said those words. And I know that's the reason he forces me to say them out loud.

I look down at my own knees, wondering how I got here. Why I gave in so easily and whether it's going to be worth it in the end. "I asked to be punished."

"Exactly," he replies. "Now look at me."

When I do what he asks, his hand moves down to his belt, which he slowly unbuckles. Then he pulls the button on his pants and zips down. I gulp when he nudges down his boxer shorts, and his cock springs out.

I've seen my fair share of men, but this … he's so huge that it almost makes my eyes fall out. His tongue briefly darts out to wet his lips, and I'm suddenly hyperaware of the fact I was staring. But my body still tenses up as he grasps his cock. What is he going to make me do? Will he tell me to pleasure him as a punishment?

He starts rubbing himself in front of me. At first it's

slow, careful, like he's taking his time to enjoy himself. And I keep my eyes on him, not because he asked me to, but because I want him to know exactly what I feel and think about him. Because I'm waiting for him to pull the trigger, get up, and fuck me.

But as the more time passes and the harder he jerks off, the more I'm beginning to doubt my own conclusions. When he stands, I take a deep breath. Here he comes.

I close my eyes and wait for the inevitable. All men eventually end up savages.

The longer I wait, the more it seems like forever.

"Look at me," he growls.

When I open my eyes, he's still right in front of me, furiously jerking himself off. His tip is right near my forehead, and I don't move an inch. His eyes are filled with fire, the kind that sets a soul alight and burns with a passion that shoots the pleasure right up your veins. And for a moment, I'm in awe of this man, this captor of mine who has taken my breath away.

His thick cock glistens with pre-cum, and it drips down onto my skin. *Drip. Drip. Drip.* I swallow when the droplet is large enough to roll down my nose and onto my lips. His hand reaches for my face, his thumb gently nudging my jaw down until my lips part, and the droplet rolls into my mouth like a salty afternoon snack.

The groan that emanates from his chest pushes all my buttons. I don't know why it affects me this much. Or why I let this man do these things to me without putting up a fight. Or why ... my pussy is flushing with heat and desire.

Fuck.

His big forearm tightens as his jerking off speeds up, his muscles bulging underneath that rolled up white shirt, and for some reason, my mind veers off into the forbidden ... imagining what it would be like to strip away those last pieces of fabric still covering his skin.

Suddenly, he stops, and I'm brought back to reality. His hard-on bounces up and down as his hands come down his side, his eyes smoldering with rage.

But why is he angry? This is what he wanted, isn't it?

He cocks his head. "Are you hungry?"

Is that a real question or a rhetorical one? And is he talking about food ... or something else?

I gulp and nod, wondering what happens if I agree to his terms. Would it be easier if I just complied? If I let my captor take control?

"Then show me ... show me how far you're willing to go ..." he says with a guttural voice that completely unhinges me.

I bite my lip and look at his dick as it bounces up and down, my eyes following the trail of pre-cum as it drips onto the floor. And I open my mouth and lean in until the tip touches my lips. His back arches, and his hand reaches for my face. I close my eyes, expecting the worst for my insolence at the table.

Instead, he offers me the sweetest of caresses, and I almost melt into a puddle right there.

I know I'm not supposed to feel this way, but my body is already faltering as I'm getting more and more confused by my own desires. And the longer he stares at me with those passionate eyes, the more I'm beginning to wonder … what if? What if I let him have his way with me?

He reaches for my hair, bundling it up into a fist before slowly entering my mouth. He takes his time sliding down my tongue, inch by inch, as though he's savoring the moment I gave in to his demands.

A devilish smile forms on his lips as he dips lower and lower until he's fully inside. I have to force myself not to gag; that's how huge he is. For a second, I contemplate biting him, but I stop myself before I give in to the thought. What good would hurting him do? It would only keep me here longer.

Instead, I stay silent and obedient like the little angel he pegs me as. He fucks my mouth, each stroke faster than the one before.

I'm completely overtaken by the control he exudes from just his eyes boring into my soul. I am powerless against him, yet I want nothing more than for this man to take what he wants. Because it is the only thing leading to my release from this beautiful, opulent prison.

So I let him claim my mouth as though it belongs to him. I let him revel in the sight of my open mouth as he plunges inside, pure lust filling his eyes. The faster he goes, the harder he grips my hair, his muscles tensing up.

I'd be lying if I said it didn't turn me on.

But I would never admit that out loud, especially not to him.

He bites his lip, and I can't help but stare right back into his eyes as he comes. A loud roar emanates from his mouth, and a spurt of warm, salty seed gushes down my throat.

He doesn't relent. Not until every last drop has slipped down onto my tongue where it's impossible to spit it back out.

"Swallow …" he groans, his dick still deep inside.

I do my best even though the feel of him there at the back of my throat makes me gag. I gulp it down until there's nothing left.

He cleans himself on my tongue and pulls back out again. But I will keep this down, no matter the cost, because that is the only answer. The only solution to all of my problems.

Submit to this man, and it'll be over soon.

At least, I tell myself that while I look at him. But he refuses to look at me as he zips back up, his face scrunched up as though he's thinking of something and doesn't want me to see. He takes in a deep breath.

Suddenly, he marches off to the door.

"Wait," I mutter as I get up from the carpet. My feet wobble as my bruise-covered knees aren't used to standing yet. "Where are you going?"

He pulls the cuffs of his shirt back into place. "I have business to attend to."

I frown. "But I gave you what you wanted."

He pauses and glances at me over his shoulder. "If that's what you think, then you still don't understand why you're here …"

He opens the door. I step closer and hold up a hand. "Wait. You can't do this."

"What? Leave?" His brow rises. "Are you going to stop me?"

My jaw drops. "If I did what you wanted, you'd let me out. Right?"

His lips slam together, and he breathes out a sigh. "Only you can free yourself."

"How?" I ask, but it sounds more like a plea.

"Admit the truth," he replies.

"What truth?"

"Stop looking for a way out, and start looking for a way in," he says.

Then he turns around and marches off.

I run to the door. "Wait. I don't get it. What do you mean?" But as the last word leaves my lips, the door is shut right in my face.

I bang on the wood. "Please! Tell me! What did I do? If you don't tell me, how will I know what to do?"

But there is only more silence to my questions and zero answers, just like before.

All I can do is slowly lower myself against the door as the tears stream down my cheek. I let myself believe that I could win this man over. By doing his bidding, by being his and allowing him to have his way with me, I thought I could make him fall. That he'd eventually set me free.

Instead, it was only more punishment.

Punishment for a crime I don't know I committed.

FIFTEEN

ELI

I slam the door shut behind me and stay put for a few moments, listening to the sounds emanating from behind the wood.

"Wait! Let me out!" she calls.

Her cries reach through and slice into my heart like a knife.

I wish I could go back in there. That I could hug her and tell her it'll all be okay.

But doing so would only confuse her ... and me.

I'm her captor, the one she should submit to. I'm not supposed to care.

Grinding my teeth, I throw my head back and force my legs to move. Away from that door, away from that room, away from that woman ... That little angel who made me sin.

I should've never gone in there. It was a mistake to think I could feed her by hand, that I could make her trust me, when I can't even control myself.

Tobias was right, and I knew it. I just didn't want to face it.

I march straight to my room, ignoring the screams coming from down the hall. I have too much on my mind to be able to focus right now. I have to calm my nerves.

When I get inside, I immediately throw the door closed and stampede around the room. It feels as though I'm practically breathing fire. I reach for a glass of water, but that won't quell the flames either, so I chuck it into the fireplace. I roar out loud and slam my fists onto the wooden door, enraged at myself.

How could I let myself slip that far?

She was supposed to be punished for her sins.

I wasn't supposed to indulge in mine.

But fuck me, those pouty lips just begged to be used. And I succumbed …

I was supposed to teach her not to stray. To obey, submit, and dig deeper and deeper until she found the answers. Until she'd see just how much she's sinned.

Instead, I was the one to lead her astray.

She thinks I'll give her freedom? Wrong.

I'm the one to bring her hell.

I slam my fist against the door again and close my eyes, breathing out a few sighs to calm myself, but nothing works.

Why? Because I know what must be done now.

After all, the sinner must be punished.

I lean away from the door and turn my head to glare at the fire churning at the other end of the room. Without thinking about it further, I rip open my shirt and tear it off my broad shoulders. Then I march toward the fireplace, grab one of the irons lying on the coals, and shove the burned end into the skin between my shoulder blades.

I roar out loud from the searing pain, the fire singeing its way through my skin. When I can't take it anymore, I drop the metal onto the floor and go to my knees with it. Burning pain surges through my veins, my eyes blurry and watery. With a fistful of carpet, I take in a deep breath and let the pain ebb out of me like a wound seeping blood. Cathartic.

"Again?"

I stay put where I am, even though I know full well who just entered my room.

"Tobias," I groan, still on edge from the scent of burned skin. *My* skin. "What are you doing here?"

"I was going to tell you the new arrivals are here, but I could hear your screaming from downstairs," he says as the door slowly falls into the lock. He sighs out loud, and I can hear from the tone he's looked at the burn. "What did you do to her?"

"Nothing," I retort as I stand straight even though the wound is still burning into my flesh. I cannot show any weakness. Not even amongst my own.

144

"*Nothing* doesn't warrant a punishment," he replies, walking in farther. "C'mon. Spill it."

I turn to face him. "It's none of your concern."

He eyes the hot iron and then the glass pieces scattered all around the fireplace. "Something the matter?"

"What do you want, Tobias?" I interject.

"I'm your right-hand man. Can't I be worried about you?" He folds his arms. "Seems to me like you're going in too deep."

"I have it under control," I reply, rubbing my eyes with my index finger and thumb. "Do we really have to talk about this again?"

"You've been acting out ever since—"

"Say it then. Say what's on your mind," I interrupt, slamming my fist onto the table. "I don't need your pity."

"She shouldn't have been brought here," he says.

I make a face and sigh. "You think that because I personally chose her over any other girl, I'm jeopardizing this House?"

"No, I know our guards are the best of the best. She cannot escape," he replies.

"Then what is it?" I step toward him. "Are you afraid I chose the wrong one?"

"I trust your judgment," he says, swallowing when I get up in his face.

"Your questions tell me that's a lie," I say.

A flicker of regret briefly flashes in his eyes.

"I'm worried about your health. About what this girl

might do to you if you don't go easy and do this gently," he says.

"I know what I'm doing." I grab the bottle of scotch from the table and drink from it without a glass. Tobias looks at me as if I've lost my mind, but I don't care. I need this to numb the pain. "She needed to be taught a lesson."

"Is this about you or about her?" he asks.

My eyes narrow. "I don't have feelings if that's what you're asking."

"Then why do this?" He points at the iron.

"Because I claimed her," I blurt out.

His eyes widen. "Already?"

"It is part of her submission," I say as I pass by him to look at myself in the mirror and the added gashes on my back that will soon form a scar. "There is no other way."

"Yes, there is," he replies.

Our eyes connect through the mirror, and for a moment in time, I imagine striking him with the bottle of scotch in my hand.

"No," I say.

"But I haven't—"

"I know what you're thinking and what you're going to suggest, and the answer is no," I rebuke before he even gets a chance. "She is mine and mine alone."

"You're obsessed," he retorts.

"That's your perception, not mine," I reply, still gazing at him through the mirror. It's easier than facing him or my sins head-on.

"You wouldn't have gone down this road if you weren't," he says. "No wonder you've done this to yourself. You've already fallen."

"It was just one slipup," I reply.

"A slipup?"

I chuck the bottle of scotch at the fire too and watch as it erupts into a fiery blaze. "I do what I need to do for this House. Do you understand?"

He nods a few times, slowly. Finally, he's gotten the message. I will not be persuaded to surrender. Not with this girl.

"I will do it. Her punishment is mine and mine alone," I say. "And if I have to sin to bring her to submission, so be it."

"But how far are you willing to go?" he asks, ogling the scar on my back. "How much of yourself are you willing to lose?"

My nostrils flare, and I grab my shirt and put it back on, pushing the button through each hole before answering him. "That is my burden to carry, not yours." Then I approach him and place a hand on his shoulder. "Now … shall we go meet our new guests?"

***

Amelia

No matter how many times I brush my teeth in this fancy marbled bathroom, it doesn't make the memory of him go away. It's not just the stain of his claim on me but my own submission that makes me want to rinse myself off over and over.

How could I be so easy? So willing?

I opened my mouth like it meant nothing, like it came naturally, and I'd done it a million times before. But no one, not even Chris, was allowed to do that. Yet I let this man, this monster, take my mouth as though it'd always belonged to him.

I can still see those hungry eyes in my mind, yearning for more as he looked down upon me, as though he wished he could do this to me every single day. As though he wanted to sweep me off my feet and carry me into the bed to fuck the night away. All the ways he wanted to use me, own me, destroy me … all in a single look.

And it mesmerized me to the point that I forgot what I was agreeing to.

That I let this monster control the narrative.

And he still didn't set me free.

Anytime I think of escape, I give in, yet when I do, it doesn't change a thing.

He won't let me out, of course not … if I'm such a gullible, controllable girl, he'd be stupid to do that. I'm an easy mark. A girl he can use to his every delight.

So why did I think that this was even a remote possibility?

His words are deceptive. They make me think that I have a choice when, in reality, he's already made that choice for me. Rules don't apply to him because he makes them.

I have to keep that in mind the next time he comes into my room.

So I stay wary at all times. Even when sleeping, I keep one eye half-open and my ears perked. Doesn't matter if I'm reading a book or if I'm soaking in the bath, I watch those damn cameras like a hawk. Any time they move, I capture which way they go to know if someone's watching or not. I've even waved and wondered when they'd come to get me.

But no one comes for hours on end, and it makes me question why I was brought here in the first place. Why would he capture me only to ignore me when he sees fit? Unless I'm truly nothing more than a plaything. Someone to beg him.

Because that's what this is all about … me asking for help, asking him to give me the answers, asking him to tell me what I did that made him do this to me. Me … finding out the truth behind my own wish.

Punish me. Two simple words I still cannot wrap my head around even though I've tried for hours to decipher my own thoughts. I've dug and dug until nothing was left unscathed, but I have no idea why I would say those words, let alone to a stranger like him.

All I remember is going to party at Club M and waking up with a hangover at the park with no recollection of what I did prior. But that happens sometimes, right? I'm not the first person to get drunk and do something stupid.

Nothing to write home about ... or punish someone over by locking them up in a tower.

But then why did he pick me?

I sigh and stare outside again at the garden beyond these walls. I wonder if he'll at least let me roam around inside them, even if just for a little while, just to get a whiff of what freedom I can have in this confinement.

Suddenly, someone knocks on the door, and I sit up straight in my lavish blue gown that I found in the wardrobe, expecting another shot at persuading Eli.

But Mary sticks her head inside my room, and the momentary buzz flooding my veins flows away like a bloodletting.

"Hey ... how are you feeling today?" she asks.

Has another day already passed? I didn't even realize.

I nod. "Fine, I guess." As I get up from the chair, she holds up her hand.

"No need. Eli is quite busy today," she replies, and she holds up a plate. "But look what I have!"

I frown. Food? "But I thought that was his job?"

"Job?" Her eyes widen, and her cheeks flush. "Oh, no, no, no. Eli never brings food."

"He did. Yesterday," I say.

With her lips still parted, she pauses for a moment. "Yes, well … that was an off-day thing. It probably won't happen again." She giggles. "As bringing food is actually my job."

Her job? Interesting. So he went against his own rules yesterday. Maybe he isn't as strict as he seems.

She bustles inside and places the plate on the table in front of me. "There you go. Bon appétit." She smiles and places a fork and knife down too. "Please be gentle with your cutlery. If you misuse it, it may end up making things worse for you."

My eyes narrow. "Misuse it?"

She finishes by setting down a glass of cola. "If you tried to use them as weapons."

When my pupils dilate, she adds an eerie smile.

"But you won't do that, I'm sure. Besides, the cameras keep an eye out for any trouble."

I gulp. She's not even afraid to say it out loud. I don't know why that surprises me, but it does.

"Now, when you're done, simply place the finished plate in front of the door and knock, and someone will come and pick it up."

"Someone?" I raise a brow.

She nods. So there are more of her … whatever she is. The point is, Eli's got help in keeping me here, which means my hunch was right. I won't escape that easily.

"Anyway … I hope you enjoy!"

She stays put for a while as I stare at her, wondering if she's going to leave or stay or do something else that'll require me to stay on guard.

She frowns and leans in to scoot the plate closer to me with a big smile on her face. "Go on."

We look at each other for a few more seconds. As I pick up the fork, her eyes follow the trail until I've picked up a piece of the chicken potpie and transferred it into my mouth.

"And?" she asks, clutching her serving tray close to her chest.

I swallow it with disdain. "Good. The cooks did their best to impress you."

"Thanks," I say as I don't want to hurt their feelings. But all of this feels so duplicitous. "So is this the norm?"

"What? This chicken potpie? No, they make different stuff every day."

I take another bite. "No, I mean, you bringing it here. Shouldn't I be eating with Eli?"

She shakes her head. "I'll be bringing you breakfast, lunch, and dinner on Monday, Tuesday, Thursday, Friday, Saturday, and Sunday."

I stop chewing. "What about Wednesday?"

"Oh, that's the day Eli requests that you eat with him."

Okay … that's odd. "Why Wednesday?"

She shrugs. "Those are the rules. I don't make them. Besides, he's far too busy to entertain one girl every single day."

I narrow my eyes and put down my fork. "Who … else eats with him on the other days?"

She cocks her head as a wicked smile spreads on her lips. "Well, the other guests, of course! Who else?"

SIXTEEN

Eli

Three new girls wait for me in the hallway. I walk down the steps and study each of them. One girl shifts on her feet as her eyes bore into mine. The other looks down at her feet, her body trembling. The third ... unmoving, absent, as though she's in another world.

I wish I understood what it felt like to be new to this place, but unfortunately, I've never had that privilege. They must be scared, worried, anxious to know what is coming. But I am not here to calm their nerves.

"Ladies ..." I say as I take the final step down the stairs and open my arms. "My name is Eli. Welcome to the House of Sin."

The first girl's brows furrow. *"House of Sin?"* She clutches her modest dress as though it makes her feel safe.

One of my aides steps out from the shadows, but I hold

up my hand. "No need to intervene."

The aide nods at me before stepping away again, but the girls noticed him, and that's the only thing that matters.

I focus my attention back on them. "This is your new home now."

"Home?" the middle girl murmurs. "But I already have one. Where is my grandpa?"

"Perhaps you only thought you had a home," I answer, gazing at her with a fire burning in my eyes.

It is not her grandfather she should be crying for. After all, he is the one who sent her here.

I start pacing up and down the hallway in front of them. "Any of you know why you're here?" When no one answers, I continue. "You're here because your parents, grandparents, or the one in charge of your upbringing or education didn't think you were capable of being saved. You've messed up so badly that they looked at me and begged me to fix you."

"Fix me? But I'm not broken," the middle girl murmurs, shaking her head. "I didn't do anything."

"Your grandparents sent you off, didn't they? After a big fight when you destroyed their most prized … *possessions*," I say. When her eyes widen, I smile deviously. It's a metaphor, but she knows what I mean. "Yes, I know all about your misbehavior."

"So what is this place then?" the same girl asks.

I rub my lips together. "Think of this place as a sort of moment of re-education."

"*Re-education*?" The first girl in the modest dress balks.

"What kind of nonsense—"

"Silence!" one of my guards growls at her, and his anger immediately makes her shut her mouth again.

She has spirit, but it's definitely been broken already. Just not hard enough.

"You're the one who came from the *Family*, didn't you?" I narrow my eyes at her when her pupils dilate. "Thought so."

That must be the one they couldn't find a husband for.

"I had a life before that cult," she says, scrunching up her face in dismay.

"I know you did," I say, looking her straight in the eyes. "But your time there is over. What matters is the here and now, and you need to learn how to control yourself, so you can live a fulfilling life."

"What will happen to me after then? Will you ship me off too?" she spits.

I cock my head. "I guess that depends on your behavior and what you manage to learn during your time here."

She makes a tsk sound and looks away with folded arms, but not before taking a deep breath. She knows not to taunt me. She's learned that much from the *Family* that she belonged to for quite some time. Keep your head down and don't talk back too much, or you might get hurt.

"So what is this then? Are you a part of that Family cult too?" she asks.

"Not a part, no," I reply with a gentle smile. "More an extension."

"I don't understand any of this," the middle girl mutters, her body quaking even more when I approach her.

I grab her chin and force her to look up at me. "You'll understand soon enough."

When I release her, she goes right back into her shell as though it's the perfect way to stay out of trouble. But this is not submission. This is fear.

Fear can be useful … sometimes.

But this House isn't about abject fear. It's about control.

To change the world, one must be willing to sacrifice one's morals and ethics for the greater good. And that's exactly what we do.

I take in a breath. "You will all be staying here for the time being."

"Why?" the girl on the left asks. "Why was I brought here? Am I going to be forced to marry here too?" Her defiance strikes me as odd for someone who came from the *Family*. Then again, maybe that's exactly why they sent her to me in the first place.

Some of them don't blend in well, and they're given to me as a last resort.

I smile at her. "You ended up here because there was no other choice. This is the last stop. For all of you." I look at all the girls, even the one who's completely distant. "This is where your sins stop."

"*Sins?*" the middle girl mutters.

I pause, focusing my attention on her. As I stand before her and lean in, she cowers before me. "*No one* is without sin."

I myself dabble in and out of sin regularly. But it is not without reason, and I too will be punished for my sins one day.

Their day of reckoning just came sooner than mine.

***

Amelia

After hours on end of not seeing or hearing a thing, a loud thud wakes me from my dreamless sleep. It's the middle of the night, and I can barely see a thing. I turn on the light next to my bed and throw off the blanket, listening to the sounds.

Another loud thud has me jolting up and down in the bed.

More banging ensues. Someone's door is slammed shut, but it isn't mine.

A woman's voice echoes through the hallways.

It isn't Mary.

There is someone else here too.

Which means I'm definitely not alone anymore.

I jump out of bed in my short black nightgown and throw on the bathrobe lying on the floor before walking to the door. I lay my ear against it and listen. Footsteps move away from the hallway and march down the stairs. Another loud bang makes me pull away, but it's not my door that's banged.

It's the one next to mine.

My eyes widen, and I step back to stare at the wall next to the door. Covered in lavish tapestries, it has a huge cabinet and a big lounge chair in front of it. With all my strength, I shove aside the chair and cabinet, throwing all my weight into moving them. When they're finally gone from the wall, I blow out a huge breath, then slam my fists against the wall … and wait.

Nothing.

So I pound on it again, and again, and again.

A knock makes me stop.

My heartbeat is pounding in my throat.

Another knock.

Violent thoughts of escaping this place rush through my veins, exploding into a tortured smile. Tears cascade down my face. I am not alone anymore, and that is both a blissful and agonizing reality to face.

"Hello?" I yell, hoping they can hear me.

But there's no response, and now I'm starting to worry. Will I ever be able to communicate with my fellow prisoner? Assuming this is even someone like me. What if it's one of them? It could be Tobias or Soren. Someone mad enough to throw stuff around and slam a door shut. And maybe they only responded to me pounding the wall to amuse themselves.

I sigh and sink to the floor, not caring about the spider webs that appeared from behind the cabinet, and I place a hand on the wall. I refuse to believe it. There's no way one of those three would have a room right next to mine. It would make more sense that they have their own wing in this giant house.

I have to believe another captive is in here—someone who needs me as much as I need them—and there has to be a way we can communicate.

But what do I do?

I look to my left and my right, but the only thing still covering the wall is a part of the long drapes in front of the windows. So I crawl over there across the dust and shove aside the curtains. Excitement warms my chest so much that it makes me want to burst into screams. Near the corner is a vent, smaller than a hand but large enough to peek through. But better yet, the cameras can't reach this spot.

I lie down on my back and turn my head to have a look. There's a small airflow tube behind it, probably to ventilate the rooms, which isn't covered by anything, so I can see straight into the other room. It's like a peephole for mice.

The thought of them crawling across my floor makes my skin crawl. But there's no point in dawdling on tiny details when something much more important is on hand.

I knock on the wall again, this time right next to the vent, in the hopes that whoever is on the other side of this wall will go to her knees and look. She knocks too, but she's not even close.

"Down here," I say.

There's some shuffling, and a wardrobe is moved. Maybe it was blocking the vent.

Then two eyes with beautiful copper irises appear out of nowhere. They stare right back at me as the pupils dilate.

"It's you," I mutter.

"Who are you?" It's definitely a girl, judging by the voice.

"I'm a prisoner, just like you," I say. "My name is Amelia. What's yours?"

"Anna," she replies. "What is this place?"

Wait, so she doesn't know either? I thought I could ask her. Damn.

"I don't know. All I know is that this man brought me here. His name is Eli."

Her eyes widen. "I know that name. That's the guy who told us why we were here."

My heart races. "What did he say?"

"Um … something about us needing re-education for our sins or something," she mutters.

Sins? So he's attempting to do the same thing to her too now.

She groans. "It's all a bit fuzzy. It all went so fast."

They must've drugged her too. "Are you nauseous?" I ask.

"No, just … confused. That's all." She sighs. "But I don't get it. I don't understand why they sent me here."

I frown. "Who did?"

"My grandparents."

I don't see her eyes anymore, but her face is still visible, along with the tears rolling down her cheeks. I touch the wall, wishing I could get closer, so I could give her a warm hug.

"I'm sorry," I murmur.

"It's not fair," she says. "I just had a big fight with them, that's all. And now I'm stuck here."

"How old are you?" I ask.

"Eighteen," she replies.

Oh, my God. That's so young … especially to be thrown into a prison like this.

"You?" she asks.

"Twenty-three," I reply, and I clear my throat. "And you're sure you're not nauseous?"

"No, why do you ask?"

I swallow, wondering if I should answer because it might only scare her more. "Nothing."

"All I know is that one minute I was at home making a cup of tea while texting my grandparents, and the next, I was in this guy's car, and they blindfolded me until I came here. I don't even know where we are or how far away I am from home." She sniffles some more, and it breaks my heart.

"I'm sorry," I mutter.

"How did you get here?" she asks. "Did your parents or grandparents give you to Eli too?"

"No …" I suck in a breath. "I …" I can't even say the words out loud.

Who would choose this?

She would curse me.

Hell, I've cursed myself over it.

How could I ever admit that I asked him to do this to me?

"I don't remember," I reply, and I look away before she decides to look at me through the peephole.

"What is he going to do with us?" she asks.

"I don't know," I reply.

"But you've been here longer than me. Don't you know what's going on?"

"I've only been here a few days, I think." Actually, now that I think of it, I don't even know how long exactly. With every hour I spend here, I feel as though time is slipping away from me, and the days have turned into numbers on a clock ticking away.

"All I know is that Eli doesn't take no for an answer," I reply.

She gulps. "What did he do to you?"

"He …" I don't dare say it out loud. Not to a girl this age. "A bunch of dirty things."

She sniffles again. "Is he going to do that to me too?"

"I know as much as you do, Anna," I answer. "There's no telling what he or any of his buddies are going to do to either of us."

"Is it going to hurt?" Her voice sounds strained. "Oh,

God …" She sounds like she's panicking when a muffled whimper follows.

"Anna, don't," I say. "Don't panic. It won't do you any good."

"But I can't be here. I don't belong here. Why would my grandparents send me here? To these men?" she says between sniveling and wiping her nose.

"What was the fight about, if I might ask?"

"I … I …" she stutters. "Fell for a boy I shouldn't have."

A boy? That's why they sent her here? That doesn't make any sense … unless your grandparents are cruel as hell.

"I never thought they'd put me here …" she says. "I don't deserve this."

"Aw, I wish I could hug you right now," I say.

She smiles gently against the opening before showing me her teary eyes again. "Thanks. I'm more worried about the others, though. They don't have a girl like you to talk to."

"The others?" My jaw drops as I gasp. "So there are more."

"Two other girls came with me. But when I was pushed into this room, I could hear two more voices coming from the rooms we passed that weren't from those other two girls."

"Six in total," I mutter to myself, trying to understand what it means.

I look up at the door and the half-eaten food still on the

cabinet.

That's when it hits me.

I was only invited to eat with Eli, Soren, and Tobias one day of the week.

The rest of the seven days are meant for them.

The only question is ... who and where is number seven?

SEVENTEEN

ELI

"YARGGHH!" The voice shrieks, and all the hairs on the back of my neck stand up straight.

I throw the palms of my hands up against my ears and grumble to myself. The instruction manual on my lap is of no use if I cannot read it in peace and quiet.

When the yelps have stopped again, I sigh out loud and lower my hands so I can continue reading. There's much work to be done, and I will need my father's teachings to know what to do.

Another scream has me sitting straight up in the chair. The book tumbles from my hand onto the floor.

"Soren!" I yell.

My eyes roll into the back of my head. The painful howls of the man are too hard to ignore, so I get up and march out of my study and head straight into the dungeon just beyond the corridors behind the stairs.

It's dark and damp in this place with only light bulb fixtures to illuminate the brick walls and ceilings, and I'd barely find my way around if it wasn't for those incessant cries of pain guiding my way.

When I finally get to the chamber I'm looking for, I fish my key from my pocket and ram it into the lock, kicking the door open as fast as I can.

Soren's whip stops midair, splattering blood across the wall. His body blocks my view, but I know exactly what he's doing.

"Can you please stop the noise?" I growl. "I'm trying to read."

Soren merely replies with a grunt.

"Thanks," I reply, and as I close the door again, another *THWACK* sound follows, but no more cries.

Good. I don't like being interrupted, especially not when I'm trying to figure out what to do.

Because no one else before me has done what I've done. No man has ever contemplated, let alone tried, to bring in a sinner who wasn't sent to us.

But I did. And now I don't know what to do with her.

The answer seems simple, but it never really is. Because for a sinner to be redeemed, there must be one to judge. There must be forgiveness. But who am I to forgive her for a sin she did not commit against me?

The other girls … they have family who sent them here. Parents. Grandparents. Aunts. Friends. Foes. Someone who thought they needed this in order to redeem themselves.

But not Amelia. No one is waiting for her to apologize. How in the world am I going to trigger her to confess?

I return to my study and sit back down in my chair, rubbing my eyebrows. There must be someone in the history of this House who has done the same, right? But no matter how many books I read about our family, the more I'm lost to the question I don't have the answers to. Because what do you do with a sinner who cannot even remember her own sin? Let alone the fact that she wasn't sent ... she was invited. She said yes because deep down, she knew she had to ... even if she cannot remember why.

But I will help her.

It's what I do best.

***

Twelve years ago

The first day I was allowed to go down the stairs into the cellar made my heart pump so hard it felt like it would burst out of my chest.

For years, my father had been teasing me with hints of what went on down there. Because I was too young, he never fully disclosed what his job was. Whatever happened behind closed doors stayed there even though I could always hear the groaning, the cries, and the whispers.

They lured me again and again to come and have a peek,

but the minute I did, Father's guards would be there to keep me from trying.

And now the day has finally arrived that I get to join my father in his work. The one thing our family has been doing for centuries. Divine work, he calls it, and the responsibility of it has been handed down from generation to generation.

And I can't help but feel as though it is finally my time to shine. My time to learn what hides behind these thick, wooden doors.

I pause in front of the stairs, the guards eyeing me up as though they're reminding me that my father can take back permission at any time, and they will intervene. I must do everything I can to ensure my father is content with me.

Just as he always says ... behave, and you will be rewarded.

It's our family's mantra. A good one, but a harsh rule to live by if you ask me.

I swallow hard as I take a step down into the cellar, where the shrieks are still audible to this very day. I've always wondered what was hiding in there. An animal? Or a monster? My imagination always ran away with me.

My father taught me there is no shame in the work he does. He's proud of his accomplishments, so I've always assumed the noise was just part of the job ... along with the pain to your heart the second you hear those screams.

But I've grown used to it. Or rather, I was forced. As someone who was homeschooled, I didn't know any better, and I wasn't allowed to know the truth either. Not until today.

And because that day has finally arrived, the tension is almost too much to take.

I walk down the stairs and go through the dark hallways lit by only a couple of lights. It's scary and damp and reminds me of a dungeon. There are several wooden doors, but only one of them seems to be in use right now, and my father is standing right in front of it.

I suck my lips inward and stop in front of him.

"Finally … it's time," he says, his deep voice always striking fear into my heart, even to this day. Not the fear of danger but the fear of sheer power.

Because my father is one powerful man. I've known that since I was a little boy. Men from all over the world would visit this giant mansion just to get some private time with my father. Not just any men, but rich ones. Ones who ruled the world.

And no one knew, of course. No one but us.

When I looked in the papers or online, no one would ever mention a word about these men all meeting here in secret. But I knew. And I relished in their power, wondering what it would take to get to where they were.

But what struck me most of all was how they all revered my father.

What was it about my father that had all these powerful men entranced to the point of them signing over whatever he asked for to take a glimpse at what he does?

It only intrigued me more.

And now that I am finally here with him as he towers over me, I can't help but feel grateful for the opportunity I've been given. But what will I find behind those doors?

"Are you ready?" he asks me.

I nod, but my back is sweaty, and my knees feel like they're about to buckle on me.

His hand rests on my shoulder, steady, squeezing tight as though to tell me to stay calm and be vigilant all at the same time.

"It's going to be hard. Unimaginably hard. But no matter what you see, feel, or hear, you must stay, and you must persist. It is the only way to learn what our family does. What we are. Do you understand?"

I nod again, but I can barely contain my own mix of excitement and fear as adrenaline pumps through my veins and makes my toes and fingers jittery.

"All right," he says, and he turns around to face the door. He casually fishes a key from his pocket and stuffs it into the lock, turning it sideways. One final glance over his shoulder and I'm unable to look away.

"Go inside," he says.

He steps aside, allowing me to get closer. I swallow and press my hand against the door. It creaks as it opens, and a bright light blinds me at first, so I cover my eyes.

"Don't look away," my father growls as he steps behind me, keeping the door open but also blocking the exit with his body.

He turns the knob on a button, and the light dims.

On the other end of the room is a man, strapped to a standing bed, facing the light.

I suck in a breath as my father says, "Go on."

I move inside with determination even though the dread sinking into my shoes makes them feel weighed down. The man on the bed groans, and I pause for a second, but my father's encouraging gaze compels me to push on.

But when I finally get to meet this man bound by leather straps, my heart almost stops beating.

His face is covered in scars, his mouth sealed tight with tape, his eyelids forced to stay open as he's been staring into the lamp for God knows how long, unable to look away, causing his eyes to singe and make him go blind.

Panic floods my veins.

"He's going blind!" I yell at my father, who approaches me.

"Yes, I know, boy," he muses as he laces his fingers over my shoulder and looks me dead in the eyes. "That's the whole point."

His words reverberate over and over in my head as I come to terms with the fact my father did this intentionally.

My whole body trembles as the man turns his head to look at me even though he's most likely lost his sight already. He groans again, jerking against his restraints, and it makes me jolt.

"Don't be scared. He can't hurt you," my father says, pointing at the leather straps around the man's arms and legs.

172

I'm not scared. I'm surprised by the sheer magnitude of my father's horrendous treatment of this man. Why would he do this? "I don't understand. Why would you tie someone up like this and make them go blind?"

He grabs my shoulder and forces me to stay put and watch the man suffer. "That's it. Let it make you uncomfortable. Let it ooze into your veins until you can no longer deny the heinous atrocities committed here."

This is what he wanted to show me?

All these years I spent excitedly waiting … for *this*?

A man suffering the most horrendous pain imaginable?

I shake my head. "What is wrong with you?"

My father leans over my shoulder, his lips thin and curled upward as he whispers into my ear, "You're asking the wrong question."

"Then tell me why," I retort.

"Exactly. Why? Why did this man deserve this pain and punishment?"

I swallow again around what feels like a ball of wool impossible to untangle. "What did he do?"

"Good …" My father smiles. "Now you're getting where you're supposed to go."

He steps out from behind me and grabs the man's chin, who immediately jerks and resists. His face contorts, but the man has no tears left to cry.

"You think that I would do this to an innocent person?" my father asks. When I don't reply, he adds, "Of course not. Men like him deserve all the pain they receive. He and so many others are part of the problem, part of the disease spread all over this earth."

"Disease?"

He turns his head back to me, wearing a vile, diabolical grimace on his face. "Sin."

Sin ... Like the church kind of sin?

But why would my father do this? There are laws in place to punish those who commit crimes. "We have police for that, don't we?" I ask.

"No!"

SLAP!

The sudden smack against my cheeks makes all the noise inside my head disappear. I've known this stinging pain for so long, yet I've never gotten used to it.

"The police merely take someone into jail. They don't make them see the error of their ways. Not even with their silly programs," he rants. "And who do you think pays the police, huh? The working class? Politicians? Only sometimes. No ... the real power lies ..." He fishes the man's wallet from his pocket and opens it up, taking out a few dollar bills. "In this."

"Money?" I ask, finding this all hard to believe.

What does money have to do with punishing the people who committed crimes? Does he get paid to do it? Is that what this is?

"People pay you to hurt others?" I try to insinuate.

When he raises his hand again, I raise mine to protect myself, and he stops midair.

He sighs out loud. "The people who own the money are in charge of this world. You think the police can do anything against those who hold the world in the very palm of their hands? Of course not," he says, averting his eyes. "They buy out their sins. They own the police."

"So what do you do?" I ask.

"I work ... for those who do not consider incarceration to be enough, for those who do not want their family's sins to become public knowledge," he answers, clearing his throat. "*We* work for the most powerful families in the world. And when they find that harm has been done, they send these criminals directly to *us*."

He makes it sound as though I already work here. As if I'm as much a part of his schemes as he is.

But I'm not sure I want any part of this.

My father quickly snags something off the table to the side, grabs my shoulder, and forces me to look at him as he stuffs it into the palm of my hand. When I open my hand and see the blade of a knife, my fingers begin to tremble.

I gasp. "No."

"No?" My father's brows rise, but not in a mocking way. It's more in a daring way, as though he's threatening me with just a single look.

But I won't be swayed. Not without proper cause. Not even when the palm of his hand could strike me at any time. I'm not afraid of pain. I'm only afraid of what it would do to me, to my soul, if I made the wrong choice.

So I lift my head high and stand proudly as I gaze at my

father towering over me, and say with strength in my voice, "Tell me what he did."

A tepid but diabolical smile spreads on his lips. "This man ..." He leans over and whispers into my ear the very words I wished I'd never heard.

Words that would make any man, woman, or child scream in agony.

Words that ignite your heart into blazing fury until it wants nothing more than to burn anything within its vicinity.

Children. Hundreds. Thousands. Used until they were innocent no more, then slaughtered like animals, leaving nothing but brittle bones for the longing parents wishing their child would come home.

Nothing. Nothing compares to this pain. Not even the searing sun blinding your eyes while your insides were pecked out by vultures.

"There is only one way to make a criminal atone," my father says. His voice shifts in a way I've never heard before, like it's twisting and contorting as he speaks, almost like a nightmare come true. And if I spoke now, my voice would sound exactly the same.

This is what he wanted me to know. To experience.

The violence, the rage, the perverted reality of our world culminating into one single moment in time when the sinner is not given a second chance, a comforting cell, time spent waiting on a clock ticking by to be free and do it all over again.

No. The pain ends now. It ends here … with me.

"Pain is punishment. Punishment for the unjust, the unworthy, so that they may confess and repent. And if not … they will burn, as they deserve," Father mutters as he pushes me toward the man, my blood boiling as my hatred seeps deep into my bones. "Now give this man what he is owed."

***

Present

With a sigh, I put my book aside and get up. Time to get to work.

I saunter up the stairs and make my way to her room. Tobias just exited another, and he gazes at me with a darkened look on his face.

"Difficult?" I ask.

"It's never easy," he replies. "Some are worse than others. Only time will tell if she learns to accept her new situation." He winks. "As will yours."

"Hopefully, yes," I reply.

"She must. There is no other choice," he replies with a deadly gaze.

I straighten my back. "I know." He's being pedantic now.

He nods and clears his throat. "I'll be downstairs preparing for the next one, so if you need me, let me know."

"I won't," I reply, and I pass him before he can say anything else.

I clear my throat and knock on Amelia's door.

She doesn't respond.

I knock again.

"What do you want?"

Not the reply I expected, but good enough.

"I'd like to talk."

It takes her a while to respond. "Why?"

"You know why," I reply.

She sighs out loud. "Fine. Come in."

I fish my key from my pocket and push it into the lock, opening the door. The moment I step inside, she immediately eyes the key in my hand.

Even if I request her permission to enter, I don't really need it, and she knows that. Asking is merely a part of the chivalry, the courting of her mind. Because what man would ask permission when he can take what he wants freely?

Her eyes sweep up to my face, and I smile in response. In her dark purple gown, she stands in front of the window with her hair braided and pale skin dotted with makeup, looking like a true princess. And I realize at that moment she is the most beautiful creature I've ever laid eyes on.

If only she wasn't here to be punished.

EIGHTEEN

ELI

Biting my lip, I close the door behind me and step farther inside. Her eyes travel away from me and out into the garden beyond the barred window. I cock my head and watch her. Her elegant posture almost vanishes into the painted walls as though she wishes to disappear. And it moves me.

I rub my lips together and approach her, placing two hands on her shoulders as she gazes out into the world beyond this small room. Her body tenses under my touch but then relaxes again the second my finger softly grazes her neck to slide aside a few delicate hairs.

I lean in to whisper into her ear. "It could all be yours."

She gasps, but before she can utter a word, I place my index finger on top of her lips.

"Don't ask how because you'll need to make a promise

you can't keep."

I plant a gentle but firm kiss on top of her shoulder as if to say … *you're mine, whether you want to be or not.*

She shudders, covering her skin with goose bumps. I peer over her shoulder at her quivering lips that just beg me to kiss them, and my eyes can't help but peer down at those perky tits nestled in that tight dress that I just want to tear off. She really made an effort to impress me today. The question is, why?

The left side of my lip perks up into a devious smile. "You dressed up for me. Did you know I was coming?"

She sucks in a breath. "I like to be prepared."

She obviously knows what's expected of her. Dress appropriately in here. Tight. Laced up. Sky-high heels. Why? Because if they wore anything else, it'd be much easier to escape.

Fancy clothes weigh you down … and they make you look pretty too.

I smile against her ear and whisper, "Smart girl."

I pet her braided hair and let it fall against her back, my hand brushing the skin behind. Every time we come into contact, her whole body tenses up, and I can't help but wonder …

My hand reaches between her thighs, toward the crevice I know is ripe for the taking. I only need one swipe along her wet entrance to know the truth.

I groan into her ear. "You really are a dirty one …"

"Do you get off on it?"

Her brazenness makes me pause. Sometimes her fearlessness even catches me by surprise.

"If you think I do this to indulge myself, you're mistaken," I reply.

She narrows her eyes at me. "Is that why you're touching me?"

Rage at her insolence bubbles to the surface, and I grab her waist and wrist and whisk her around in my arms, locking her in place as she hovers on one foot. "Do not mistake my kindness for weakness. Do not play games with me, Amelia." I lean in to press a kiss on her chest, right below her chin. Then I look up into her shocked eyes. "Unless they are of the sexual kind."

She swallows, visibly shaken. "Please …"

"Please what?" I mutter, my grip on her wrist still firm.

"Take what you want … Do what you like. I don't care. Just … let me go," she whispers.

I cock my head. Finally, she says what she's truly thinking.

"You think I'm going to take you for myself?" I whisper, my finger still wet from her pussy. "That this is all just so I can have my way with you?"

I admit I have thought about it. Many, many times, in fact. But I cannot let my lust control me. The sinner must be punished. Those are the rules of our House.

"You enjoy it, don't you?" she hisses back.

A filthy smile forms on my face. "Would you prefer the lie or the truth?"

She swallows and tilts her head, and my eyes and lips are immediately drawn to her skin. Inching forward, I graze my lips on the skin underneath her ear, and her lips quake from anticipation.

"I'd do it again if it means you'll submit," I whisper, pressing a soft kiss onto her skin. Her legs squeeze together. She's probably thinking about it just as much as I am. "If it means you'll get closer to the truth."

"I don't understand," she mutters.

My nostrils flare. "You being here isn't for me. It's *for* you."

Tears well up in her eyes again. "But why would I ever want this?"

I lower my gaze to meet hers. "Because your soul craves redemption."

She shakes her head, and I set her on her feet again. Pushing her to face the mirror, I place both hands on her shoulders. "Look at yourself. Look at how you dressed up. All to win my approval." I lean over her shoulder to whisper into her ear. "My desire is not more important than your soul. And it feels guilty." I touch the skin around her neck, just above those ample tits I wish I could free from their bonds. "This heart begs to be released from its chains."

"How?" she asks.

"Think," I reply. "Remember what you did, and you will be free."

Her pupils dilate as though something is being brought to the surface of a deep dark lake that she's trying to wade through. But beneath the shallow shore lies an ocean of depths that she has yet to explore. And that's exactly why we're here.

"I'm trying. I swear," she replies. "But I'm coming up blank."

I narrow my eyes. "Think hard."

"I did," she says, rubbing her lips together. "Please, can't you just help?"

"Help?" I cock my head and look at her through the mirror. "Only you can help yourself."

"But you know what I did that made you want to put me here," she replies.

I grab her chin and force her to look at herself. "Look at yourself. What do you see?"

She swallows. "A girl … lost by a single word she should've never said."

"Is that all you see?" I ask.

She just looks at me as though she has no clue what I'm talking about. "So ignorant of your own beauty, your own strength." I slide a few strands of her hair aside and caress her cheeks. "No amount of ugly bruises can erase that."

Her brows furrow, and her hand rises to touch her face. Does she only now realize how gorgeous she is without the scars of her past?

"They're gone …" she mutters, staring as though she's seeing herself for the very first time.

"Exactly. *He* can't touch you here," I say. I'm not going to say the name of that pig out loud. I'd rather focus on her.

"Look at that girl in the mirror. Look at how far she's come."

"Far?" she scoffs. "Into a gilded prison? Chris is still at home, waiting for me," she says. "He needs me."

"No, he doesn't," I reply, wishing I could erase him from her mind.

She furrows her brows. "He'll come to save me."

"He won't do that either," I retort.

Her lip quivers. "What do you mean?"

I smile and look her dead in the eyes. "I gave you what you asked for. You begged me to punish you."

"But why did you choose me?" she asks, completely ignoring what I say.

"That's not the right question, Amelia. The right question is, why did *you* beg me to?"

She fights the tears staining her eyes. "I don't know."

My fingers dig into her skin. "You have to tell me. It's the only way."

Her face darkens. "I can't remember!"

***

Amelia

I'm losing the fight for control over myself. After that ungodly yell emanated from my throat, the tears flowed freely across my cheek and down onto that expensive purple dress I took so much care in putting on.

I did all of it just to impress him, to make him want me and seduce him into taking me … so I could slither my way into his heart and slowly convince him to let me go.

But nothing is going according to plan.

And the longer I stare at myself in the mirror, the less I recognize.

"Think hard, Amelia," he says. "Think about that night. When you went out to party all by yourself. What happened?"

"I don't know. I think I went home, and …" My eyes search the mirror for clues, but I'm coming up with blanks. "Nothing. I can't remember. I don't know what I did. Or what happened after. I only remember I woke up in a city park in the middle of the night."

I can't remember what happened between, and that scares me more than anything.

My body starts to shake vigorously, my eyes growing bigger and bigger. "Why can't I remember?"

Panic flushes through my veins.

Suddenly, Eli spins me on my heels and wraps his arms around me. I'm overcome by the sheer force of his grip and the tenderness with which he holds me as though he wants nothing more than to calm the storm brewing in my heart.

But why? Why would someone like him even remotely care about me?

He put me in this situation. He made me say those words.

Why can't I take them back?

Why can't I ... undo what I did?

My heart pounds in my chest as images from that night flash in and out of my mind like paintings appearing and vanishing in a split second. Me entering my apartment. The bruises I tried so hard to hide. The kiss I shared with Eli.

I almost choke on my own saliva, but Eli only buries me further into his chest, forcing me to come back to the here and now.

"Don't let go," he says.

Of him? Or reality?

Right now, I'm not so sure.

But the memories flashing through my mind make me feel weak. Vulnerable. Exposed.

More than any kind of sex could ever do to me.

And it wounds me.

I look up into his eyes, those hauntingly beautiful eyes that undo me, twist me, unravel me at my core. Who is this man that seems to know my deepest, darkest secret, one I don't even know myself?

I swallow. "I'm sorry."

I don't know why I say it. Or why I want him to hear it.

The smile of a gentle master appears on his face. "I'm proud of you, angel."

And he cups my face and presses a kiss to my forehead. A kiss that warms my heart and makes me forget, just for a single moment in time, that I am not who he thinks I am.

He leans away and grabs my arms, pushing me back so he can look into my eyes. "I think you're ready now."

"Ready for what?" I ask.

"More."

My cheeks turn crimson red. "More … of you?" I don't know why my mind instantly goes there.

But he immediately snorts. "No, Amelia." He tips up my chin. "But rest assured that I will take from you what I desire when necessary."

I gulp, my body instantly flushing with heat. "I thought you didn't want—"

"Oh, I want you. Make no mistake, I've wanted to bury my cock inside your sweet, wet pussy and make you mine since the very first day I saw you."

The sheer filth of his words makes my jaw drop, and my eyes widen.

"But I didn't bring you to this House for that. I brought you here to repent," he says, and for some reason, the excitement in my body deflates a little. Still, the way he stares into my eyes as though he means business makes me forget. "And you're well on your way."

"How?" I mutter. All the ways he's made me come flash through my mind again, and I cross my legs to stop my pussy from thumping. "Are you going to force me to put those panties on again?"

A wicked smile spreads on his lips. "I have plenty more in store for you …"

I gulp at the thought.

"But first, I think a reward is in store."

My brows rise. "*Reward?*"

"For your courage. For trying to face the impossible," he says.

"I don't understa—"

His finger on my lips interrupts me. "You don't know, but you will. Eventually, everything will click into place. And when it does, you'll thank me for it."

Thank him? I'm not so sure about that.

"What do you want more than anything?" he asks.

"Freedom." The word slips out of my mouth before I realize it, and I almost want to slam my hand against my mouth. I shouldn't have said that. What if he tries to punish me again?

But instead of rage, there is only kindness in his eyes, and it confuses me.

"I'm not the monster you think I am. And if you behave, I will let you explore."

My lips part, but I can't even form the words I want to say.

He's letting me … out.

"Not the world." He grabs my shoulders and makes me look at him again. "This House. And if you misbehave, you'll lose that privilege. Do you understand?"

I nod a few times, completely overwhelmed by my own deranged happiness over the slightest form of freedom, however small it may be.

"Good little angel," he replies, and he pecks me on the forehead again. "It'll all be easier if you just give in."

NINETEEN

Amelia

A few days later, I'm invited for breakfast once again. I put on my big girl panties and dress up accordingly, knowing he'll appreciate the effort. Even though I'm a prisoner, I can at least try to fit in with what he expects. If I play along and go easy on myself, maybe there will be an opportunity later. Even if he says he won't fall for me, there is no guarantee. He's a man, after all, and every man has an inner beast waiting to be released. His just happens to be chained well. But he's shown it to me once, so he can show it again. And when he does, I'll be ready. I'll woo him with every ounce of my soul until I can spin him around my finger and convince him to let me out. Or at least, give me more freedom until he's finally gotten from me what he so desperately wants.

I wish I knew what it is that he wants me to tell him, what's hiding inside my own mind. But how could I tell someone what I don't know? Is there a way to find out?

I gulp, thinking about what he told me, about how he will force me to tell the truth, one way or another. What will it take, and how far will he go?

And how much of myself will I lose in the process?

I let out a sigh and wait in front of the door. Only one way to find out.

When someone pushes a key into the lock on the outside, I know it's time.

My heart begins to race. The door opens, and Mary greets me with a smile.

"You look lovely today," she muses, looking me up and down. Her comment makes me blush. "Red? Provocative."

I shrug. "Fits the occasion."

She nods. "Can't fault you there." She beckons me. "C'mon."

We walk down the long hallway again, and I can't stop myself from staring at the doors where I know the other girls are being kept. A part of me struggles not to interfere and bang on those doors in an effort to let them know I'm here and that I won't abandon them, even if I'm Eli's personal favorite.

But another part of me knows I won't get anywhere if I break the status quo. If I let my emotions rule, the guards standing by will immediately intervene, and I will have accomplished nothing.

No, the only way to win this war is to face it head-on, no matter how painful, twisted, or deviant it gets.

"Eli is really excited to see you," Mary suddenly says as we approach the staircase.

I pause. "How come?"

"I don't know, actually. Maybe it has something to do with your conversation?"

I suck in another breath as images of his hands on my shoulders and his lips on my skin invade my mind. Goose bumps scatter on my skin. "It was nothing."

"That can't be true," she replies, raising a brow. "Eli never gets excited about anything." Her smile grows. "You seem special to him."

My eyes widen, and my hand touches my chest as though I can feel my heart beating out of it.

Special? Me?

That can't be right.

She quickly heads downstairs. "This way, please."

She points me in the right direction, the same room where we had breakfast the last time. Or at least, they did, because I wouldn't dare touch it.

I guess some things have changed.

"Thanks," I tell her.

Not because I'm grateful, but because getting some extra points with her can never be a bad thing. I need to keep my enemies close.

When I enter the room, the three of them are situated at the back of the table again. They all look up at me, three deadly and possessive stares that make my heart pound in my throat. But Soren quickly looks away, and Tobias returns his focus to a newspaper as though everything is fine and dandy, and they aren't keeping seven people captive.

But maybe he doesn't realize I know.

Soren's already munching on a piece of bread that he plucked out of the basket while he picks at a wound on his knee. He doesn't even seem to notice I'm here, which is a good thing, I guess.

After a quick breath to collect my nerves, I approach the table and sit down. Eli never takes his eyes off me, and it makes me blush even more than before.

"I'm glad you decided to join us," he says. "Are you hungry?"

I nod. I'm not up for another bout of starvation if I can prevent it.

Besides, I doubt he'd want to poison me after all the trouble he went through to keep me locked up here.

I sit down on a chair near the edge of the table in the same place as before.

Eli narrows his eyes. "You sure you want to sit there?"

My lungs suddenly feel constricted. "Do you want me to sit somewhere else?"

He smiles. "Smart girl ... answering a question with another question."

I make a face and fold my arms. "I learned from the best."

Tobias snorts. "You've got a tough one on your hands."

"Tell me about it," Eli responds. "But I knew that when I found her."

"Let's just eat, shall we?" Tobias suggests.

"Of course," Eli responds as he leans over the table and stares at me while blinking a few times. "Wouldn't want our guest to wait."

He keeps taunting me, and I don't know why. It's almost as if he's trying to make me turn to rage and despair again.

He claps his hands, and the servers enter, carrying plates filled with delicious fruits, yogurt, breads, butter, and condiments, as well as hot plates of bacon and eggs. When the smell fills my nostrils, my mouth waters.

They place the food on the table and a few drinks such as orange juice and coffee, and I can't help but stare at the food, wondering when I'll be able to dig in. But I don't know if I can.

I look up. Eli's still staring at me, a devilish smile appearing on his face. It's almost as if he's enjoying the sight of me waiting for his approval. Like a dog ready to be fed.

"Go on ... Enjoy," he says with a certain kind of glee in his voice.

I pick up one of the fruity yogurt cups and drop in my spoon. Then I grab my fork and pick up a strawberry, shoving it into my mouth on full display, taking ample time to chew. He watches my every move, and when I swallow, so does he.

Tobias simply sighs and throws down his newspaper.

"Enough. Get a room, you two."

Eli turns his head to him and frowns. "To do what, exactly?"

They look at each other now, full of unbridled testosterone waiting to be unleashed. And it brings a smirk to my face. A tiny bit of power is back into my own hands, even if it's useless and leads to nowhere. At least I can enjoy the two having a fight. Is that so wrong?

"Torturing our guests is not part of breakfast. Or lunch. Or dinner," Tobias replies.

"No," Eli muses. "That's reserved for the times between."

My jaw drops, and the strawberry I was about to eat falls off the fork and onto my plate.

"We'll leave the torturing to Soren," Tobias says.

Soren merely grunts and snags an already peeled egg off the big plate, which he stuffs into his mouth whole, and then rips some of the bacon to shreds with his teeth.

"Right." Eli returns his attention to me. "Are you enjoying the food?"

How can I reply when they so easily talk about torture right in front of me?

"I … Um …"

"I suppose it's not poisoned now, is it?" he asks, raising a playful brow.

I close my mouth and stare at him for a few seconds before I decide to play along with his game. If I can't get through this without being challenged, then I'll face him head-on.

"Who knows, maybe you've only laced some of the fruit," I retort, and I tear a grape off the stem and glare at it for only a moment, long enough for him to see, and then chuck it into my mouth and chew on it provocatively.

"She knows you well," Tobias muses, and Eli thrusts his elbow into him to shove him off the table.

"Enough," Eli growls. "Amelia. Eat."

He picks up a few strips of bacon, an egg, and a few pieces of bread for himself, taking a big bite from the egg.

"Woof," I reply, which makes him stop halfway through chewing.

Tobias bursts out into laughter. "You sure picked the right one, didn't you?"

I pick up a cupcake and happily munch away on it.

Eli throws him an enraged look. "Tobias, please don't insult our guests."

"Oh, I'm not insulted," I reply, and I grab an egg too and shove it in my mouth, chewing and swallowing. "On the contrary, I'm amused."

"Amused?" Eli cocks his head while Tobias just frowns and then continues eating his breakfast.

"Oh, yeah … being locked in a golden tower is quite amusing," I retort, and I grab a few grapes and chuck them in my mouth.

Tobias almost chokes on his coffee, and Eli throws him another maddened look.

"All right, all right." Tobias raises his hands and then

picks up his plate and coffee. "I'll see myself out." He gets up from his chair and marches toward the door. "I have enough to do today."

When he's gone, only Eli, me, and Soren are left, but he's not let out a peep since he swallowed down the egg.

Eli now focuses his attention on him.

"Soren. Would you do us a favor and eat …" Eli pauses. "Somewhere else?"

I don't know what he meant to say when he said nothing instead, but it's caught my curiosity.

Soren stops chewing his food and looks over at Eli with hatred. Then he loudly scoots his chair back, gets up, and steals a few more buns off the table before stomping off.

"Thanks," Eli adds, but Soren doesn't reply. He merely grunts like a bear.

I don't think I've ever heard him speak. Can he? Or does he just refuse?

I shift in my chair as I glare at all the food left behind … and how little my stomach can suddenly handle now that we're by ourselves. Eli won't stop staring at me.

"Why did you ask them to leave?" I ask.

He picks up his fork and knife and elegantly cuts off a piece of bacon. The way he shoves it into his mouth captures my attention as though he's chewing off a piece of the pig's soul, and it makes me swallow.

"Because I prefer to be alone with you," he replies.

My whole body tingles.

"I thought these breakfast moments were meant as a

way to introduce me to them," I reply, the chair suddenly feeling very uncomfortable even though I'm as far away from him as possible.

He takes another bite of his bacon and looks up at me. "It's merely tradition. Nothing else."

"Tradition. So you do this sort of thing more often?" I ask. "To other people?"

His eyes narrow, and he places his fork down on his plate. I guess I've hit a chord. "Bold of you to ask so many questions when you know what's at stake."

Rubbing my lips together as my stomach does a backflip, I think about all the possible outcomes if I try to nudge him a little farther to expose the truth. "I'm merely trying to understand."

"I've told you everything you need to know for now," he replies.

"You want me to give in, yet at the same time, you won't give me anything in return and no leeway."

He plants his hands on the table, spreading his fingers as he gets up from his chair. The menacing look on his face makes me wonder what he's going to do … and maybe regret that I ever spoke up.

He suddenly marches over to me and puts his hands down on the table right in front of me until we've locked eyes. "Do not mistake these moments of calm for kindness. When I choose to let you eat with us, I can take that privilege away again with the snap of my finger," he says.

I just stare back at him without saying a word.

"I can put you back in your room and let you eat by yourself for all eternity. Is that what you want?"

I shake my head, willing the tears to stay away. "Please, don't. I can't take being alone for so long."

He reaches for my face, and the moment his skin touches mine, electricity shoots through my veins as he tips up my chin. "I wish you would just accept what I gave you without so much a fuss," he muses, giving me a smile. "But I guess that goes with the territory of finding a girl like you."

"Why?" I mutter.

"Because you weren't brought to me. You weren't given. You came willingly," he says, leaning in so close I can feel his breath on my skin. "And that is priceless."

I suck in a breath as he lingers close to my lips, the mere thought of him kissing me making my whole body shiver. I don't know what I'm feeling, whether it's excitement or fear or all of it at once.

"You don't even know how special you are …" he whispers. "And just how hard it is for me not to give in."

The top of his lip touches mine, and I want nothing more than for him to kiss me. Not because I crave it, but because it will make him crave *me*. Because it will give me leverage when I have none. At least, that's what I tell myself as his lips hover dangerously close to mine.

"Then why don't you?" I whisper back, opening my mouth, ready to let him take me.

Suddenly, his eyes burst open, and he leans away, staring

at me as though I'm the devil himself.

His eyes narrow as he shakes his head. "You try to seduce me …"

"I'm not trying to do anything," I retort, folding my arms.

A smirk forms on his lips. "Don't lie, angel, or I might have to punish you."

My eyes widen, and my cheeks become as red as the strawberries on my plate. I don't know what he has in store for me, but it can't be good, so then why is my pussy thumping all of a sudden?

His hand slides off the table, and he stands again, towering over me as I sit here in this chair like a submissive.

"You will be permitted to roam this House. The locked rooms are prohibited," he says, straightening his back as though he's forcing himself to forget he was just about to kiss me. "And don't go near the corridor behind the stairs."

He marches off, and I quickly get to my feet and turn to ask, "Why? What's in there?"

He pauses and glances at me over his shoulder with a smolder burning in his eyes. "Hell."

TWENTY

Eli

I lock myself in my room and take a few deep breaths. I even slap myself in the face, but nothing works. Nothing I do can chase away the thoughts of owning her. Claiming her. Using her for my every dirty desire.

And I admit, I have had many of those thoughts swirling through my head.

From the moment she came here, she's been in my every waking thought. My desire to take her has only grown since. Nothing I do—not the punishments I dish out nor the conversations we have—can douse the flames burning inside.

And I knew this going in, but I never imagined it would hit me this hard or that I'd find it impossible to stay away.

The problem is that I can't. I need to be the one to make her admit the truth behind her lies. But it'll cost me my sanity in doing so because for her to come clean, I must become a sinner. And who will be the one to punish me for all the sins I've collected since I brought her here?

Will she be the one?

I go to my knees in front of the cross on my fireplace and strike one on my chest, saying a prayer. There is no right or wrong answer to this. There is only the path which I must take, and I must finish what I started.

Sighing, I get up and go to my desk, opening my laptop. I bring up the camera app and check out each of them until I find her floating gracefully across the halls in her beautiful gown. One I bought for her, specific to her size and measurements. I knew exactly what to get, and I must say that she looks stunning in each one. I can't get enough of staring at her beauty, wishing it was mine and mine alone to enjoy.

She's exploring each crevice of every room in this House, as though there are secret passages to uncover. I smirk to myself as I look at her thin frame and pretty posture, taking wicked pleasure in the fact that I'm watching her. My cock already strains in my pants at the thought of all the filthy ways I can break her after she's broken my rules.

Maybe not now, but eventually … she will. And when she does, I'll be right there to catch her during the fall.

**

Amelia

I look behind the curtains and even shove aside some of the furniture, but nowhere do I find another one of those vents like the one in my room. This begs the question … do they only appear in the bedrooms?

I wish I could find out, but I reckon the doors are locked tight to keep the captives from escaping. And besides, I'm not nearly done exploring this House and its huge corridors. There is so much to see. Each room has its own designated purpose; there's a room for inviting guests, whoever those may be, with lounge seats and tea sets, the kitchen in the back with staff slaving away each day on the most delicious of meals, the scents of which delight me when they enter my nostrils. In the back is a relaxation room with what looks like games on top of a shelf. Then next to that is a room with windows leading to an underground pool, and I can't help but feel in awe at how much this place reminds me of a hotel.

All the luxuries but none of the freedom to use them.

There's even a huge library with giant bookcases on two different levels. I want to steal one of these and bring them with me to my room. Maybe he'd allow me to read them all.

What am I even thinking? Why should I care what he allows?

I sigh to myself. Even when I'm on my own, I think about the repercussions of my actions. About the consequences he'd force onto me.

But if I don't, something bad could happen to me, and I'm not sure I'm willing to risk that.

I look around the room and search for the camera until I've found it. Someone's watching me, I'm sure. Whether it's him or a guard, someone is making sure I stay within these walls and don't touch anything I'm not supposed to.

I wonder where the footage is. If I could ever see it.

If he's watching me right this very second.

And at that moment, I decide to stick up my finger and flip the camera the bird.

Suits him right.

Even if I can't do what I want, even if I can't escape … this tiny rebellion will be my way of standing up for myself. I know it doesn't do anything, but at least I've made my point.

I don't like him. In fact, I despise him. Every handsome inch of his body exudes power and control, traits I do not possess … and I envy that. I wish I could be half as arrogant as he is and get away with it. That I could do whatever I wanted without there being anyone to tell me no.

Maybe I would've told Chris exactly what I thought of him when he betrayed me.

Maybe he would've begged me to forgive him.

Not that I care. He doesn't care about me either. If he had, he would've come looking for me.

Has he even noticed I'm gone?

My teeth grind against each other, and I force myself to forget him as I turn around and make a swift exit from the library.

Even if I'm being watched, I can't give up on trying to find a way out, no matter what it costs me. If I'm going to be punished anyway for something I can't even remember, then at least I can try to wriggle my way out of it all.

Besides, I'm not done exploring yet. This place is like a giant castle with plenty of nooks and crannies. I walk along the staircase and stop and stare at the corridor behind it. The one Eli told me not to enter. What could be hiding there? Something forbidden? Or an escape?

My heart palpitates as I take a step toward it, unable to curtail my curiosity. But I hesitate and stop right before I step over the edge into the corridor.

If I do this, he'll punish me.

Or worse.

He might take my one happiness—going outside my room—away.

He's done it before. He could do it again.

I don't want to risk it.

So I step away again and sigh.

Maybe I'll have the courage to disobey him someday, but not now when I've only just grasped a tiny bit of freedom.

I turn and walk up the stairs, determined not to let anything get in my way again. If I can't explore down there, at least I can try to find an exit up here. Maybe one of the doors is still unlocked. If one of them has a balcony, maybe I could slip down the railings and use some of the greens growing up against them to flee.

My escape plans are always so elaborate, and my fantasy is running away with me. Because I know none of that could ever happen.

He'd catch me before I'd even try.

But how could I just … give up? Impossible.

So I rummage every door I can find, hoping at least one of them remains open.

I even try the ones right next to my bedroom. Those where the other girls are housed.

I frantically rummage at the door handle, but none of them opens.

"Hello?" someone calls out.

It's not the same voice as before.

I plant my ear against the door and call out. "Hey. Are you there?"

More rummaging is audible, then someone slams against the door. "Who are you?"

"I'm not one of them. My name is Amelia."

"Are you going to help me?"

Panic rushes through my veins as I look around, searching for the cameras or any guards keeping watch, but they're all downstairs.

"I can't," I reply. "I don't have a key."

"You're messing with me. Why would you come here if you don't? How did you even get out?" the woman asks.

"Wait. You're lying. You're one of them, aren't you?"

"No," I reply. "That's not—"

"Stay away!" She pounds on the door, and I jolt back in shock. "You're trying to trick me!"

Has her mind been eroded that much just from being locked inside?

"He told me I'd be seduced by sin. I will not let you do this to me! I don't need more punishment."

"I'm not here to punish—"

"Leave me alone!" she squeals, and I take a step back, tears welling up in my eyes.

She's completely lost inside herself. In her mind, I am part of the problem. I'm here to make her feel like she's sinned.

But I'm not. If only she could see. If I could just remove this damn door, she'd know, and I could tell her and show her the truth.

I have to find a key. Eli, Tobias, and Soren must all have one. But what about … Mary? What if I could steal it from her unnoticed?

If she comes into my room and brings food, I could sneak close while she's picking up the laundry. Maybe it could work.

I grumble to myself and focus on the next door, hoping that the other girl is more open to talking. Of course, this door is locked too, but the keyhole is at least large enough for me to peer through. Maybe by talking, I only scare them more. If I just take a look to see what they're doing, I could find out a way to help from the outside. It beats doing nothing, right?

So I lean over and peek through the small opening, hoping to catch a glimpse of a girl as lonely as I am in this ivory tower.

Except what I see makes my jaw drop and my heart stop.

Tobias is inside. There's a girl with long black hair strapped on a pedestal, her legs spread. Her mouth covered by some kind of strap-on … while he fucks her in the ass.

No tears stain her cheeks, and no pain mars her face. No, it is pure and utter lust making her eyes roll into the back of her head.

How could this be happening?

How could a girl brought to this place be so into all of it? How could she enjoy what Tobias does to her without repercussion and without remorse?

Suddenly, her copper eyes bore into mine. The same eyes I peered at through that hole in my wall. It's her. The girl I've been talking to.

I gasp in shock and quickly step back from the peeping hole, completely horrified by the way my own body is turned on at seeing Tobias ravage her.

But my shock is overshadowed when I step back and bump into someone.

"Going somewhere?"

TWENTY-ONE

Amelia

Eli's voice makes me spin on my heels. Too late. He's grabbed my shoulders and pinned me to the wall.

"What are you doing here?" he growls.

"I was just ... I was—"

He leans in. "Sneaking around, trying to catch a glimpse of what it is that we do."

I shake my head. "No, I was just trying to understand."

A smirk forms on his lips as though he's enjoying the thought of catching me in the act of sin. "Of course, you were. You weren't at all ... snooping around to try to find a way out."

I try to move, but he's far stronger than I am. I'm no match for his physique, and now he's got me right where he wants me.

"Let me go," I hiss, trying to free myself, but his grip on my arms only grows stronger.

"You cannot run from this, Amelia," he says, leaning in to look me in the eyes. "And you cannot deny what you saw in there."

My lips part, but I don't know how to respond. What does he want from me?

"You want to see more? Let me help you," he says. He pulls me off the wall, fishes a key from his pocket, and shoves it into the lock. After throwing the door open, he grabs my wrists, pins them to my back, and shoves me inside.

I stare at the scene before me, shame pooling in my stomach. Tobias looks up, but he doesn't stop fucking her. Anna cannot even focus her eyes on mine because she's so far gone into the scene.

Eli pushes me up against him, holding me in place. Then his breath is near my ear. "This is what you wanted, right?"

I shake my head and look away, but he grabs my cheeks and keeps my head straight in her direction. "Don't look away. Look at her. Look at that girl so desperate for relief."

Anna's eyes momentarily home in on mine as a moan vibrates through the object stuffed inside her mouth. My face scrunches up as a mixture of guilt, shame, despair, and rage wash over me. But most of all, the worst kind of emotion floods my body as she is claimed right in front of me; heat.

"Do you see now the unraveling of a human being?" he murmurs into my ear, sliding my hair aside as I suck in a breath. "See what it does to her? And to you?"

"No," I whisper, shaking my head as tears well up in my eyes. But I'm only trying to deny the truth that's right in front of me.

"You think she wants to escape?" he muses. "You think she'd accept it if you offered her a chance?"

"Yes," I whisper. But that too is a lie. Her eyes tell me she'd never.

"Or are you just scared to admit the truth? To see with your own eyes what lust can do to a human mind? How easily it breaks?" he whispers, his hand snaking around my belly and up to my breast.

He fondles me in full view of Anna and Tobias, who give no attention to the fact that we're even here watching them. But worse is the fact that the more Eli touches me, the more I want him to continue, to take me, to make me yield.

Why?

"What are they doing to her?" I ask, wishing I understood, but the more he fondles me, the more I'm losing control over my own body.

"This is her punishment."

"She doesn't deserve this," I retort, but I can't even say it without slurring the words.

"You're just like her," he murmurs into my ear, peeling away my dress from the top until my nipple is almost exposed. "A sinner always desires more."

I shake my head, but my body betrays me as he grips my thighs and shoves his hand between my legs. The more he touches me, the more I wish I would just stop fighting, that I would just give in, because it would be so much easier. Let him have his way with me. Let him take and take until I can only moan and beg for more.

"Your warm, wet pussy tells another story," he groans.

Suddenly, he rips me away from the room and throws me back into the hallway. I stagger against the banister, my breasts almost falling out of my dress as I suck in the oxygen. Eli slams the door shut to Anna's room, then grabs me by the arm and hauls me to mine.

"Wait, no," I say. "Please don't put me back in there."

"You should have thought of that before you went snooping," he growls, and he throws open the door and drags me inside, shutting the door behind him with a kick. He throws me down onto the bed and says, "I told you to stay out of our business."

I crawl up. "You only said not to go near the corridor underneath the stairs."

He paces around in front of me. "And did you listen?"

My lips part, but I don't know what to say. I don't want to give myself away.

He frowns and stares at me for a moment, rage marring his face. "Stop. Lying."

I nod, swallowing hard.

"You aren't innocent," he adds. "And neither is she."

My pupils dilate. "But what did she do to deserve that?"

He scoffs. "That's none of your business."

He sighs and rubs his forehead, pacing around again until he finally stops and points at me with his index finger. "You squandered your privilege."

Suddenly, he turns and marches off, and I shriek. "No! Wait! Don't leave me here, please!" It sounds more like a cry. "I promise, I won't do it again."

He pauses at the door for only a second, a hand clutching the doorjamb, fingers digging into the wood. After giving me a single glance filled with agony, he storms off.

***

ELI

I go right back into my chambers, but as I slam the door shut, nothing can quell the storm raging inside my head. I grab the nearest lamp and smash it to pieces against the wall. The noise makes me come to a full stop. I stare at the damage I've caused and the pain I've instilled in both our hearts.

It's been right in front of me, and I've been too blind to see.

I'm growing weak.

Easy.

Vulnerable.

And if there's anything I don't like, it's that.

But the way she looked at me, so full of despair, made me pause. I wanted her to be punished for snooping in our business, but when she realized what was going on, it was like all hope had left her.

And then she turned to me with that look in her eyes that completely destroyed me.

The minute I caught her, I had wanted nothing more than to strip her in front of Tobias and Anna, to claim her right there and use her in any way I saw fit. But that look … it undid me, forced me to come face-to-face with my own actions. With my own sin.

I saw in her the things I wished never to see.

And it hurt me.

Why?

I knew what I was going to do and why I was there, yet I still couldn't go through with it. I've lost my touch.

I go to my knees and pick up the shards, but one of them cuts into me. I stare at my hands as they shake with rage, and droplets of blood drip down onto the carpet.

This is what I'm supposed to do. Punish the weak, the insubordinate. This is my purpose in life. How my father taught me to live.

Yet … when I look at her, all of that unravels right in front of me.

Maybe Tobias was right. Dragging someone into this House solely because of my own selfish needs may not have been the smartest idea.

Still, I can't go back.

This is the way it is now. There is no going back. Not from any of this.

She is mine, and she will suffer for her sins.

As will I.

***

Amelia

For hours, I just sat there with my head buried between my knees, my hands covering my ears so I wouldn't have to hear the noise coming from next door.

Tobias went on for hours, banging her well into the night.

Who could go do that for hours on end?

I've never heard of anyone fucking for so long. Unless they did it multiple times.

I swallow hard as images flash through my mind of Eli touching my breasts, fondling my pussy, and the aching need inside to be taken and used.

Why would I ever want this? Why would I ever claim to like it? I don't understand what's wrong with me.

Unless … he's right.

Unless … I do, deep down, want to actually be

punished.

I shake my head and mutter, "No, no, no."

It just can't be true. I would never … right? I'm a good girl. He even calls me an angel. I've never done anything bad in my life. At least, not as far as I know.

There are just … hours missing from my mind.

Hours I can't seem to get back, no matter how hard I try.

Only two things are going to help me now. Either find out what I did by talking to Eli and convince him to tell me with whatever means necessary… or try any way to make a grand escape out of this place. And is that really a choice?

Biting my lip, I force myself to get up from the floor and approach the wall. I put my ear against it, but no sounds are audible. It's like the whole place has gone completely silent.

Then I hear a whimper.

Anna?

I hurry to the little opening underneath the vent and shove aside the furniture I'd put back in case someone came into my room and saw. I go to my knees and whisper, "Anna?"

The only sound is my own heartbeat.

Then some rustles as the curtain is shoved aside.

"Amelia …" she mutters.

"Is he gone?" I ask.

She nods. Then she starts to bawl. "I'm sorry."

"Hey, " I reply, wondering how she's doing. "It's okay.

You don't have to apologize."

"I said something I shouldn't have," she says.

"It's not your fault," I reply.

When she cries even harder, I slam the wall.

"Listen to me, what they're doing to you is not your fault. Do you hear me?"

"But it is!" she yelps, sniffling. "I begged him to."

I pause and lean back, completely confused. Why would she ask that? Who would want this? And then I remember … I did the same thing. It's so sophisticated, this scheme, that I don't even notice it happening right in front of me.

"He came into my room and made me talk until I gave him what he wanted …"

"Sex?" I ask.

"The truth," she replies. "And I couldn't stop myself. Once he started touching me, I just lost it. I completely lost myself." She sighs out loud. "I don't understand," she mutters, breaking out in tears again. "Why did I say all those things out loud?"

"Shh … it's okay," I say. "Don't cry. You did what you had to do to survive."

"No, that's not why I let him," she retorts, sighing. "I did it because … because …" She hiccups and shifts on the floor. "Oh, my God, look at me. I'm a mess."

"I'm sorry, I made everything worse," I say, wishing I could hug her.

I can't imagine what's going through her mind right now. So much guilt from all that pressure. The desire to escape is so strong she'd do anything to get out, even let Tobias fuck her. And I don't blame her. I'm on the verge of doing the same thing with Eli.

"I can't believe I did all of those things," she says.

"You made the right choice for you," I reply.

"No, I didn't," she suddenly barks. "Don't you see? I deserved this!"

"What?" I frown. "Stop telling yourself that."

"We ALL deserve it!" she yells, gazing at me with her tearstained eyes. "Why can't you see that?"

I don't understand what's gotten into her. "No, this is what they do to you. They trick you into believing their lies."

Her eyes widen. "NO!"

In shock, I lean away, terrified to look at her when she's so angry.

"Tobias cares about me. The only liar here is me," Anna says in a single breath.

I lean over again, but the curtain is suddenly swathed over the hole, blocking my view.

"Anna?" I mutter. "Anna? Talk to me."

"I can't. He told me this is how it's supposed to go," she replies.

"Tell me why," I respond.

"No. He forbade me from talking to anyone about this. My sin is my own to carry."

I hear footsteps moving away from the hole, and then nothing.

"Anna?" I call out, but there's no response.

I bang on the walls, but there's no one banging on them back. No matter how many times I call out her name, she refuses to come and speak with me. And it hurts. So much that it makes tears well up in my eyes again.

He got to her. Just like that. He fucked her until she caved and gave them everything they wanted. Was it even true, what she told him?

I shiver as I get up from the floor, suddenly feeling cold to the bone.

I've lost my only sliver of humanity. The one girl I could finally talk to is shut off from reality. And all I have left is my own crazy thoughts whirling inside my head, convincing me I too am guilty of a crime deserving of all this punishment.

I'm tired of sitting around and waiting. No more.

If I can't count on anyone, not Eli or Chris or even Anna … then I will count on myself.

I will be the one to set us both free.

TWENTY-TWO

ELI

Tobias groans out loud when he pulls the metal from his leg. Blood seeps from the wound, which he quickly covers with bandages and tapes it up.

"Looks gnarly," I say.

"It'll heal," he responds as he walks past me and grabs a glass from the cabinet. "Man ... I'm thirsty."

He turns on the tap and runs water into the glass.

"I can imagine after doing all that," I retort as I sip my coffee at the bar.

He chugs it down in one go, sets the glass on the counter, and then stares at me. "It took quite a bit more effort because of your girl."

I look away and sigh. "She needed to learn her lesson."

Soren stomps into the room, eyes cold as though his mind is completely shut off. He opens the fridge to take out a carton of milk and slurps down the entire thing, then throws it into the trash from a distance and burps out loud.

"Can you not?" I say, pointing at my mug. "I'm trying to enjoy my coffee here."

"That's what happens when you interfere with our work," Tobias replies, and he folds his arms. "You even tell off Soren nowadays."

"You both make too much noise," I retort.

"Do you have any idea how hard I've been working on cracking that one?"

"Really?" I raise a brow. "Because it seems like she only got here recently. If I wasn't so busy myself, I'd say you had quite an easy time convincing her to tell the truth."

Tobias smashes the glass down onto the sink. "Really? That's your answer?" He rolls his eyes. "You let your girl roam around the House."

"Yes. That's my decision, not yours," I say, clearing my throat. "Now if you'll excuse me, I have some calls to make."

When I walk to the door, Tobias blocks my way, and the air suddenly grows thick with animosity. "Something you wanna say to me?"

"If you hadn't let her out of your sight, maybe she wouldn't have snooped on us," he says, folding his arms.

"She needed to see to know what would happen," I say.

When I try to pass him, he blocks my way again.

"You make my job harder than it should be," he says. "Why?"

"Your girl was easy," I hiss. "You broke her in no time." I snap my fingers. "Like that."

"And you think yours isn't?" he retorts.

My nostrils flare. "I know she isn't. Now get out of my way."

I march past him, determined not to let his anger over me busting in on their affairs with Amelia ruin everything we've worked so hard for. Fighting isn't part of our agreement. And these boys know we're in this together.

"Maybe I should have my way with her then," he says.

I pause, right in the door opening.

One. Two. Three.

Fuck.

No amount of counting numbers in my head will quench this thirst for blood.

I march right back at him and get right up in his face. "Don't you fucking dare."

"Why not? If she's so difficult, maybe it'll finally break her, and then we can get it over with."

"She is mine. Mine, you hear me?" I growl.

"Sounds like you have a problem dealing with your own sins, not hers."

"She is a fragile thing. If you challenge her too hard, she will break beyond repair," I say through gritted teeth. "So unless you want to go against protocol and actually risk losing one of our guests, I suggest you keep your mouth shut."

We're bumping chests now, and if lightning could strike

between our gazes, this whole place would've burned down by now. The fire burning inside me is ready to burst into a crescendo. The only thing holding me back is our history together.

"The rules were put in place for a reason," he hisses.

"And I was the one to inherit them. You think you can do a better job than me?" I growl back.

"Stop."

We both look up.

It's the first time Soren's spoken up in ages. Neither of us takes his words lightly, even when there are so few of them.

Soren steps closer. "Do not forget your sins," he says, eyes boring into mine.

I gulp. He's right. We're succumbing to the very thing we swore to fight.

I sigh and lower my eyes, nodding as I take a step back. "Look at us. Look at what this is doing to us."

Tobias places a hand on my shoulder. "I don't like fighting with you. We are all brothers in this House. We should be in this together. Us against the sinners. Even when we sin, we do it together." He points at his wound. "You should never have taken her. More than anyone else, you should know that it's just not worth it."

I shrug off his hand. "*She* is."

His judgmental gaze feels like daggers in my back. "You're not thinking clearly. You can't even let us help."

"I need to do this on my own," I say.

"Why? What's so important about her?"

A pang of guilt festers in my heart, but I lock it away deep inside my chest.

I shake my head and look away, refusing to answer.

"Fine. So be it." He scoffs. "You want to do it all by yourself? Have at it. But don't come running to me when you fail. When you lose everything that matters to you. This House. This Family," he growls, but it sounds more like a cry in pain. "She'll ruin you."

"She won't," I say, balling my fist. "Not until I've ruined her first."

"Sir!" A guard suddenly comes storming in from the hallway.

"Yes?" I turn around.

The man leans against the doorjamb, one hand resting on his knee as he breathes heavily.

"What is it?" I say. "Spill it."

"Two girls …" he mutters between breaths. "They're gone."

"What?!" I shout, and I march toward him and grab him by the collar. "What do you mean *gone*?"

"Their doors were opened," he replies.

Tobias comes forward too. "How?"

"I don't know," the guard replies. "I was just taking a leak, and then suddenly, they were opened. I checked. The girls are nowhere to be seen."

Rage fills me up to the point of boiling over, and I roar out loud and shove the man aside. "Get out of my way."

I storm outside and run up the stairs, skipping several steps. Even though my back hurts like hell, I ignore the pain in favor of getting there as soon as possible. Soren is right behind me while Tobias limps up the stairs, still in pain from the metal device buried in his thigh for quite some time.

I rush through the hallway and stop in front of Anna's door. It's wide open, but there's no one to be seen. I take a few steps forward and gaze into Amelia's room through her open door. Drawers are opened wide, and the mirror is smashed, shards of it lying scattered across the floor. She's gone. Vanished into thin air.

"Oh, no …" Tobias mumbles, his voice strained and weak as though it hurts him to see Anna is gone.

And I know just who the culprit is. Only one person would even try to get away with this insanity.

My hand balls into a fist. "Amelia."

What the hell did she do?

TWENTY-THREE

Amelia

A few minutes ago

I stare through the keyhole, waiting and waiting until the guy guarding our doors finally leaves. Within seconds, I've rushed across the room and grabbed everything I need. I wrap my dress around my fist and punch the mirror until it shatters, and I gather a few of the shards and tuck them into my pocket. Then I grab a few bobby pins from the drawer in the wardrobe, and I shove them into the lock.

It takes a long while, but I've been practicing on the lock for quite some time now. Whenever I was alone, I would try to make these pins work because it beat re-reading books over and over. That was Eli's biggest mistake ... thinking I would just sit and wait for him.

Being here on my own might've mentally broken me down … but I've only gotten more and more cunning because I'll do anything to escape this predicament.

And I know Anna is just as desperate. She may not think it, she may not even say a word to me, but I know deep down she never wanted any of this.

And if she's already lost, it's on me to save her.

That's what good people do, so that's what I'm gonna do.

I poke at the lock, hoping, praying it'll work. I've waited so long for this moment, and the guard is finally gone. It has to work. It just has to.

CLICK!

The sound makes me jolt back. I stare at it for only a second. Then a beaming smile pops onto my face.

"Yes!" I whisper to myself.

I rip out the bobby pin and tuck it into my other pocket. Opening the door feels like magic, like I've done something no one else ever has, and it feels so damn empowering that I could shout it off the rooftops.

But I have to stay quiet, play it cool, pretend I'm still in my room and that nothing is going on. I don't want to alert the other guards who are still walking around. One of them saunters up and down the stairs regularly, and I need to stay out of his sight.

I only have a few more minutes left before the guard who normally walks these halls comes back from his toilet break. This was a big one. I know because I've watched him all this time to figure out his schedule—when he pees, when he eats, when he relieves himself, and when he changes shifts.

I know everything I need to know in order to make a swift escape. So I quickly go to work on Anna's door, jamming the same bobby pin inside. It only takes me a few seconds to get this one too, and when the lock pops, my heart begins to race.

I swiftly open Anna's door and burst inside, shutting it behind me.

She's lying on the bed, but her eyes are open, and she leans up when she spots me.

"I thought Tobias was coming to—" she mutters.

"It's me," I interrupt, trying to keep my voice down. "Amelia."

Her eyes widen, and she sits up straight, her black locks falling over her shoulder. "Amelia?"

My eyes water, and I nod. "Yes. I'm sorry I didn't come sooner."

"But how?" she asks, shaking her head as though she's utterly confused. "I thought only Tobias had a key?"

"They all have a key," I reply, and I hold up my bobby pin. "But now I have one too."

"That's not a key. How did you …?" Her pupils dilate. "What's your plan?"

"Escape," I say as I approach her bed and grab her hand. "C'mon."

When I try to pull her up, she resists and jerks her hand away. "No, I can't."

I frown. "C'mon, Anna, we don't have time for this."

"I can't leave," she says, folding her arms.

What's wrong with her? "What? Why not?"

"Tobias told me to stay. Said I needed this," she replies.

"Tobias is a liar. They all are," I spit back.

She makes a face. "But you don't know him. How could you say that?"

"I don't need to know him. They trapped us here, Anna. We're prisoners."

"Only because we deserve it," she replies.

I grab her shoulders. "Anna. Stop. This isn't you. I just know it isn't."

"You don't know me either." She looks me dead in the eyes. "This is what I need."

"You can't be serious," I say. "Look at me. You don't deserve any of this. You did nothing wrong, you hear me? Those men are monsters, and they are using you for their own pleasure."

"But … Tobias is trying to fix me," she says, licking her lips as she looks away. "He told me this is what needed to be done."

"They're making you believe what they want you to believe. You have to trust me," I say.

"I have to listen," she says as a tear rolls down her cheeks. "You don't know what I've done …"

"It doesn't matter, okay?" I say, forcing her to look at

229

me by matching her movements so our eyes connect. "Whatever you did, it's in the past. You've been punished enough."

She shivers. "I don't know …"

"I do," I reiterate. "You deserve to be home with your family. Remember your boyfriend?"

Her eyes light up. "My boyfriend?"

"Yeah, he's waiting for you," I say. "He wants you back home."

"But he—"

"C'mon," I say, and I grab her hand again and pull her up from the bed.

"Wait," she says as I drag her to the door. "What about my things?"

"Leave them. None of it is yours. It's theirs. Now, c'mon." I drag her through the door before she can say anything else to delay us.

I check the clock hanging from the wall. The guard's almost on his way back. There's not much time left. Certainly not enough to open the rest of the doors and free the other girls. I spent too much time talking Anna into it. Damn.

I sigh to myself and close my eyes for a second to refocus. No time to dwell on my decisions. This is what I chose, so now I have to see it through.

"Follow me," I say, looking at her over my shoulder. "And stay close."

We walk toward the staircases, but I make sure not to

take the main ones. We wait until the guard has his back turned to it before swiftly passing it. There is an elevator in a room just beyond the hallway to the right. A tiny one that ends up in a storage room next to the kitchen, which they use to get carts with food up and down.

I know because when I was allowed to roam the House a little, I made sure to check for alternate exits. Eli really should have known that letting me drift around freely would come back to bite him in the ass.

I may not be strong, and I may be a mousy type of girl, but I am resourceful. And there is nothing I won't do to get my way.

So I string Anna along for the ride and press the buttons to go down. Sweat drips down my back as we wait for the elevator to arrive on the ground floor. Anna squeezes my hand tight, and we look at each other. I fish my shard of glass from my pocket and hold it up.

The doors open.

I'm ready to fight, but luckily, we're alone.

I breathe a sigh of relief and step out with Anna following suit.

It's only a small room with one exit. Not at all a safe space to be for two wanted girls on the run, but it'll have to do. I wasn't ever going to go down those main stairs with all the guards lined up, ready to jump us. This was the only other option. That, or somehow finding a way to destroy the bars on the windows and making a grand escape there. Not the greatest idea.

"Wait here," I whisper to Anna. "If they come … hide in the elevator and go back to your room."

She swallows and nods. "I just hope this will work. I don't want to anger Tobias."

I pray the same, as I definitely don't want to get on their bad sides. We just have to get far enough away from them so they can't catch us anymore when they find out we're gone.

My hand pushes against the door, opening it just a tiny bit. I peek through and spot two cooks stationed at the far end of the room chopping vegetables for a soup.

It's now or never.

I glance back at Anna and beckon her to come.

With one big push, the door opens wide right as Anna grabs ahold of my hand.

We run across the room to the other side of the kitchen, where a door leads out back into a garden. The two men haven't noticed us yet, as they're too busy chatting and making noise with the pots and pans. So I push down the big door handle and make our great escape.

The fresh outdoor air hits me like a brick, and I suck in a breath as we run. The grass tickles my bare legs, but I pay no attention to it as we head for the forest right in front of us. I don't know where we're going, and I don't even care as long as it's as far away from this House as possible.

"Where the hell are we?" Anna asks as we run into the woods.

"I don't know," I reply. "Eli never showed me how I

got here. I was drugged."

"Right," she responds. "But what's your plan?"

I shrug as we move through the woods, the bright sun lighting my path. "I don't know. But there must be a road somewhere."

"What if a wall surrounds the property?" she asks.

I pause among the fallen leaves because I hadn't even thought about that yet. I swallow back the nerves. "We'll think about that when we get there."

I continue running, but Anna remains put. "But what are we gonna do if there is? What if they find us first?"

The panic is starting to show on her face. I have to pull her out of it.

"Don't think about it," I say, and I go back to grab her hand. "You're here with me now. I'm going to get us through this. You just have to trust me."

"Okay. I'll try." She nods a few times, and I turn around again and make sure she follows me. I don't want to lose her. I spent way too much time trying to save her, so now I have to push through and make it happen. I have no other choice. This is it.

However, these pumps are really starting to wear me down. Grunting, I tear them off my feet and chuck them away. "Good fucking riddance."

Anna pauses and giggles. "Why didn't I think of that?" She quickly rids herself of her high heels too.

"We have to be careful, though. Barefoot can be dangerous, so be aware of where you step," I say. "Let's go."

We run through the forest together, across the many puddles and dead leaves that rustle beneath our feet. We jump over thick logs, which is hard when you're wearing an extravagant dress. And I don't think it's a coincidence we had no other outfits to wear. These clothes definitely weigh us down.

Suddenly, I hear a crackling noise behind me. The noise makes me glance over my shoulder.

Two eyes catch mine. My breath falters, and my throat clamps up.

It's a guard.

What feels like minutes is actually mere seconds before the guy starts running toward me.

I don't think twice and run like hell.

"Get back here!" the guy yells at me.

"Run!" I squeal at Anna.

The sheer terror in her eyes is too much to take, but I can't console her now. We only have one shot to make it out. We have to escape this man before he catches either of us and alerts the others.

Suddenly, I hear his voice. "I got eyes on the two. Over."

"What's your twenty? Over," another voice replies.

The scratching noises every time someone speaks reveals what it is. A walkie-talkie.

"Forest. North. Headed toward the beach. Over."

Beach? There's a beach?

"Copy that. Over."

My heart beats in my throat at the thought, but I have to calm myself. It could be a riverbank.

No time to think about it. I keep running across the mossy floor, and I even jump over a few rocks just to stay ahead. Every time I look over my shoulder, he's a little bit closer, and it only pushes me to run faster. Adrenaline rushes through my body, forcing me to stay in the here and now and to keep going no matter what.

Anna is right in front of me, a few feet away, her ragged breaths filling the air with panic. One glance over her shoulder, and she's infected me too.

"Behind you!" she yelps.

I don't even have to look to know. He must be close.

I run so hard my feet become numb, narrowly escaping the trees in my path. In a few seconds, I've managed to pass by Anna. I glance over my shoulder to see if the man is still catching up.

But the earth suddenly disappears from underneath my feet.

I shriek.

Tumbling down, I try to catch myself, but it's no use. I land headfirst on the ground.

Dizziness overtakes me. My eyes feel like marbles rolling across the floor as the earth spins around me. Two feet jump down next to me.

There was a cliff. How did I not see it in time?

"Amelia!" Anna calls. "No! I need you!"

"Run!" I growl, barely able to see straight from the fall.

"I can't ... I can't do this without you," she says, her pitch fluctuating. "We were supposed to flee together."

"You can still flee," I reply. "Now go, before he's here!"

"But I'm all alone ..." she says, clutching a tree as she considers her options.

"You can do this. I know you can. I believe in you. You have to free yourself." I muster the last bit of my energy and shout, "Don't look back! GO!"

She hesitates, staring at me for a second. Then she runs off into the distance.

I groan from the pain and the whirlwind of emotions flooding my brain. I was so close ... so damn close to escaping, but I didn't look in front of me, and that was my greatest mistake.

And as I rise to my knees, the guard who was chasing us finally catches up with me.

He shoves me right back into the dirt and growls, "You're not going anywhere."

TWENTY-FOUR

ELI

I won't let anyone in this House rest until Amelia's back in my clutches.

No way I'll let her escape. Not ever.

We've come way too far, made too much progress, for it to all end now.

And if she escapes, Lord knows what she's going to do. A girl like her is volatile. She doesn't know what she did, which makes it all the more dangerous if she manages to get out. If she doesn't know the truth, no one else will. She'll endanger my business, and I can't let that happen.

So I grab some cuffs from my cabinet and head out for the hunt.

Ever since I took Amelia and brought her into this House, I've wanted nothing more than to indulge myself in a delicious chase.

Too bad this one might not end in devious sex … but in tears.

***

Amelia

The man grasps my wrists and pins them to my back while I cough and heave as he sits down on top of me.

He fishes the walkie-talkie from his pocket and talks into it. "I've got one of them. Amelia. Over."

"Copy that. Owner on the way to your location. Over."

Owner? As in … Eli?

As the guard puts his walkie-talkie away, I use my last bit of energy to wriggle my way out from underneath his grasp and fish the shard of glass from my pocket.

Without thinking about it, I shove it straight into his throat.

He gurgles and yelps in pain, his hand immediately rising to cover his throat.

My pupils dilate at the sight of all that blood oozing from his neck. I'm frozen in place as he grasps at his throat, blood pouring down on top of me. The glass shard stuck in his throat glistens, and in the light, it sometimes resembles a knife instead. I blink a couple of times, feeling as though the life is being choked out of me.

I quickly shove him off me and crawl away, my heart pounding. He falls backward into the dirt, struggling with his own mortality. For a second there, I feel guilty. Heinous for what I've done. But I tell myself I had no choice. That I had to do this in order to free not just myself but Anna too.

She's waiting for me. I have to go. Don't think, don't feel, just act.

I scramble up to my feet and stumble away. My foot feels sprained, and every step hurts, but I keep going. I can't give up. I won't give up. Because if I do … it means I'd admit that he won. That Eli's right about me. That I deserve this. That I did something terrible that deserves all of this …

And so what if I did? Who is he to judge me?

With renewed energy, I focus on finding my way out of this forest even though it hurts. My lungs suck in the air like nothing else as I go on as fast as I can, despite the fact that I can't run anymore.

I can't afford to wait until the pain subsides. The guy behind me must be coming to. He'll be right behind me in no time. I can't get distracted again.

I push forward until I get to the edge of the forest. There's another drop-off, but this time, I search for a softer slide, and I go down butt-first.

Only when I land do I look up … and my jaw drops.

This is not a riverbank.

It's an actual sea.

My heart sinks into my shoes as the panic comes to a

boil.

"No, no, no, no," I mutter, tears welling up in my eyes as I stumble around, looking for another way.

But there is only water … for as far as the eye can see.

What do I do?

"Fuck!" I scream.

I don't swear often, but when I do, I mean it.

I look out onto the horizon, wishing a magical boat would appear out of nowhere. That's when I spot Anna. My eyes widen.

She's wading right into the water.

With nothing to hold. No raft. No boat. Not even a plank of wood.

Nothing.

Just her against the waves crashing into her body, threatening to swallow her whole.

"Anna!" I call out, trying to run to her, but I'm not quick enough.

She's disappearing fast.

"Anna! Stop!" I yell, pleading with myself in the hopes that she doesn't go any further.

THUMP!

I'm coughing into the dirt, my face buried in the sand.

Someone toppled me right into the ground.

A knee pushes into the small of my back, and then my wrists are locked in place with cuffs.

I'm turned around on my back. But it isn't the guard whose eyes are staring back at me. It's Eli's.

"Where is she?" he growls at me.

"I don't know. She went into the water by herself," I reply.

His eyes widen, and he scans the surface of the water to find her.

While he grabs his walkie-talkie, I try to free myself, but it's impossible. The cuffs are too strong for me.

"Tobias. Need you here. Beach. Anna's going in. Over," he says.

He tucks the walkie-talkie away again and shoves me back against the sand.

"Why?" he growls, the look on his face so full of rage that I don't even dare to look at him.

All I can think about is how I've failed. I did everything right, planned it all out, knew exactly what to do … and then I fell.

"What were you even thinking, huh?" he growls. "Did you really think I'd let you go?"

I shake my head and slam my lips together, refusing to reply.

"Amelia." When he says my name, the tears start to run.

I thought I'd be free. That I'd make it out alive.

And now my time is running out.

"What did you do?" he asks. "What did you tell her?"

"Why does it even matter?" I mutter. "You caught me. It's over."

"She's in the water, goddammit!" he yells, looking up to scour the water again. I've never heard him swear before.

Suddenly, Tobias springs out of the forest and runs past us. He's like a lightning bolt, that's how fast he is. Without saying a word, he rushes straight into the water.

Is he going to look for Anna? I don't see her anywhere. She stepped into the water, and then I was pounced down. I couldn't see a thing. And now she's gone. Vanished. As though she never even existed in the first place.

And it suddenly becomes hard to breathe.

"You see now?" Eli whispers into my ear. "Do you see what you've done?"

Tears roll down my cheeks, sand sticking to my face. "No. We were going to escape."

"Escape is impossible," he says. "I told you that on day one. But you wouldn't believe me."

"Tell me what this place is," I reply as we stare each other down. "Tell me where I am. You owe me that."

His eyes narrow. "I owe you nothing after what you just did." He gets up and grabs me by the arms. "On your feet."

He drags me up until I'm standing, keeping me in place in front of him.

"You put not just yourself in danger but Anna too," he says. "You don't even know what you've done."

"I freed her," I say through gritted teeth.

I'm just hoping she made it out alive.

"You think you freed her from blame? From the guilt etching a gaping hole into her heart?" he hisses, and his grip on my arms tightens as he pulls me closer to his body so he can whisper into my ear. "You don't know everything there is to know."

"I did what I had to do to get us out of there," I growl back.

"And you think she needed that?" he retorts. "Wrong. If you knew what she did you wouldn't blink an eye to save her soul."

I throw him a look over my shoulder. "You're wrong."

He grabs my throat with his free hand and tilts my head up. "She's here because her world has given up on her. You think what she told you is the full truth? That her grandparents sent her here over a lover boy?" He scoffs, snorting. "She'd be vilified if she was out there. In jail. Or worse. *We* saved her. She is punished for her sins here."

"What sins? What could be so bad that you and Tobias had to lock her up and fuck her?"

Finally, it's out there in the open. Finally, I said it out loud.

The only thought on my mind.

Why are any of us even here?

It's quiet for a few seconds, the only sounds surrounding us are the birds singing songs in the trees and the waves crashing into the beach. In the distance, Tobias resurfaces from the deep, carrying a lifeless body in his arms. Anna.

Eli's grip on my throat and chin forces me to watch.

"Look at what you've done."

"She wanted to flee from your House," I hiss back.

"No … Don't you understand? She was trying to kill

herself."

My pupils dilate.

"No, that can't be right. Anna would never."

Why would she ever do that? She has no reason to.

"You pushed her to run. To escape the guilt that's drowning her," he says. "All of you deserve to be here, including her."

"Why would she do that?" I mutter, my body shivering, not from the cold but from the sheer realization of Anna's choice.

I can try to deny it all I want, but I saw with my own eyes what she did.

Even when the waves crashed into her, she kept on walking.

Even when she knew there was no escape from this wretched place, she still went for it.

She knew it would kill her.

And she still chose death.

The final words from his mouth undo me. "Her boyfriend was after her money, but she didn't see it. Instead, he made her believe her parents were the enemy. And in order to be with each other …"

I can finish his sentence without thinking about it with a single breath. "She had them killed."

TWENTY-FIVE

ELI

The second she realized what Anna had done, what her boyfriend did for her, Amelia stopped struggling. Like a meek little lamb, she gave in to the restraints and allowed me to take her away. As Tobias carried Anna out of the water, Amelia's eyes grew solemn. Like the light had snuffed out deep inside her.

And I'd be lying if I said it didn't sting.

Despite the fact that it's much easier to bring her along when she doesn't fight for control, the sheer defeat in her eyes still managed to crack the outer shell around my heart.

She should never have tried to escape.

As Tobias passes me, clutching Anna so close to his body, he throws me a single, maddening look. And I pause in my tracks, staring after him with both admiration and rage. I'm not the only one who has fallen in too deep. It's not just the House that's at stake anymore.

"Follow me," I bark.

I'm not in the mood or have the patience for niceties.

All kindness went out the window the moment she decided to run. And to bring Anna along, of all people.

Besides, it's not like she has any choice in the matter. Everywhere she goes, she's watched. If she tries to leave now, I'll catch up in no time. And she won't be doing anything foolish with those cuffs around her wrists anyway.

I continue walking with her right behind me, determined to bring her back to the House safely and keep her there. How did she even manage to get out of her room in the first place?

"I'm sorry …" she suddenly mutters.

I glance at her over my shoulder. Those are not the words I would have expected to come out of her mouth after this ordeal. "Apologizing will do nothing."

"I know," she says, averting her eyes.

I raise a brow. "Then why persist? Do you think it will make me go easy on you?"

She swallows. "No. But I hope it will make you go easy on *her*."

My lips part, but I don't know how to respond. She's throwing herself under the bus for Anna? Even after everything I just told her?

I stop in my tracks and look at her over my shoulder. "You don't need to concern yourself with her."

"But I do," she says.

"Why? Why do you care?" I ask. "I told you what she did."

"Everyone deserves forgiveness." She looks up at me with doe-like eyes, and it hits me just how beautiful she is when she's pleading for someone else's life. Of course, she'd see the innocence in people, no matter how depraved they are. She's too good for this world. Too good, even for me.

I shake it off and force myself to keep walking, despite wanting nothing more than to grab her and kiss her right there on the spot. It wouldn't be right. She isn't ready yet. She's still guilty. She cannot be mine until she's no longer consumed by sin.

"What is this place?" Amelia asks as we move back into the woods.

"The Isle of Judgment," I reply, scaling up the rocks.

I reach out with a hand to help her up, but she leans back, her eyes like a hawk. "Isle of Judgment?"

I expect she'll laugh about that name, but I wasn't the one who came up with it. My family has owned this property for generations.

"This is an island?"

Well, that's not the question I was expecting, but I'll take it.

A smirk spreads across my lips as I grasp her arm and pull her up to me, her body crashing into mine. "Yes, an island surrounded by water. There is no way to get off this island. No way ... unless you do exactly as I tell you." I cup her face and make her look at me. "You'll be a good little angel from now on, won't you?"

Her muscles tug at her top lip, her body straining against mine as she fights the idea of giving up control. But it is already far too late for that.

Suddenly, she loses her footing, and the rock beneath her foot crumbles. She almost falls, but I catch her just in time and pull her back. Her body is tight against mine, her face pressed against my chest.

"I'm curious ..." I say, and I wrap my arm around her waist and pull her even closer. "How did you manage to get out of your room?"

"Like I'd ever tell you," she hisses, narrowing her eyes.

"I think you will," I murmur as I lean in. "By the time I'm done with you."

Her whole body shudders, and I can almost taste the rage seeping from her lips, begging me to kiss and fuck them all at the same time. Because even when she says those things, her body leans closer to mine and her lips tremble with greed.

But now is not the time.

I grab her arm and drag her back with me. "Come. We're going home."

It takes a while for us to get back to the House, especially when she digs her heels into the dirt several times, to no avail. Nothing will stop me from bringing her back to my domain where she belongs.

The longer it takes to convince her of her sins, the more she's starting to struggle. It's about time I pulled the trigger and really showed her what I'm capable of. What I'm willing to do to get her to confess.

I bring her inside and shut the doors tightly. The light wanes from her eyes like curtains closing in front of a window. I take her upstairs and ignore the guard pleading for mercy as he stands near the stairs. I will deal with him later.

I push Amelia forward until she's back in her room, which has been tidied as much as possible by my assistants, including Mary.

"It will take a while to clear up the mess you made," I say as I take off the cuffs.

After rubbing her wrists, she stands in the middle of the room and stares at the broken mirror. The guard I found on my way to her had a piece of it lodged inside his neck where he lay there, bleeding out.

Her bloodied hands rise, and she gazes at them, shivering harder and harder.

I should leave. I shouldn't be here to witness the unraveling of the only girl who has ever managed to persuade me to care. But I am, and I cannot stop myself from stepping closer.

"I didn't mean to kill him," she whispers.

I place a hand on her shoulder. The air in the room grows thick with unspoken words.

When the moment has passed, Amelia sighs, tears filling her eyes.

"Tell me what you're thinking about," I say. "You can

speak freely."

She looks down at her feet. "Anything I do or say will cause punishment. Either to me or to others. It is all my fault. My fault he died. My fault that Anna almost …"

"Every action has a consequence," I interject.

She averts her eyes. "You said that before, and I didn't believe you …"

"I was only trying to warn you," I say, sighing when the tear rolls down her cheek.

I slowly spin her on her heels and make her look at me. I pick up the tear with my thumb and look at it for a moment, wondering how such a little droplet of water can have such immense effects on one's soul. And more specifically, mine.

Which is why it hurts so much to say this. "But I cannot let this go."

I turn and walk away.

"Eli!"

Her call makes me stop. I look at her over my shoulder, one foot out the door, the other still inside her room.

"How much longer?" she asks.

"As long as it takes," I respond.

The darkness returns to her eyes, that same darkness that appears every time she realizes she cannot get out of this, no matter how hard she tries.

But something has changed.

A whisper deep down in her soul, chattering words she never thought she'd hear from her own heart.

She's not innocent.
She never was.

***

Amelia

Anna has stopped talking to me entirely. Every time I go to the vent and peel the curtains away to say something, there's no reply. I've peered through the hole, and all I see are curtains time and time again. It's like she completely forgot I'm here too.

I don't know if she's upset with me because of what happened. If she blames me for not succeeding. If she wished Tobias hadn't saved her.

All this time, I thought she wanted to be freed, that she wanted to be rescued and taken from this place, but maybe her mind was already too far gone. She only wanted to disappear.

And now she has what she wanted.

She's alone in her room … all by herself, just like me.

This room … it's caving in on me. And the only reason we're both stuck in these rooms again is because of me. I wish I never tried to escape.

I throw myself onto the bed and bury my head into the

pillow, screaming so loudly my voice becomes hoarse. It's the only thing that provides relief, and as I close my eyes, I am able, for a moment, to drift away in daydreams of books and vacations, far away from this House.

Suddenly, someone rummages at the door, and I lift my head. The daydream vanishes, and my heart begins to thump in my throat as the doorknob twists.

Scrambling to my feet, I pat down the bold black and red dress I put on today and comb through my hair with my fingers so it doesn't look like a tangled mess, right in time for the door to open.

I shouldn't be excited. Shouldn't be remotely happy about someone entering this door. But solitude does something to a human being. It makes them yearn for contact ... any kind of contact ... no matter if right or wrong.

When I spot Mary's foot, my heart stops palpitating, and I breathe out a sigh.

"Hey there," she says, a gentle smile on her face. "How are you feeling today?"

"Lonely." The word slips off my tongue before I realize it. I wish I could swallow it back, but it's too late, judging from the bigger smile on her face.

"I can imagine," she replies, and my cheeks immediately flush.

"I didn't—"

"It's fine," she interjects, raising her hand. "It happens." She steps inside for a moment. "I'm sorry, I wanted to talk to you when I came to clean your room, but Eli specifically told me not to."

I sigh. "Figures."

She rolls her eyes a little. "It can be quite frustrating sometimes." She suddenly giggles. "Oh, look at me, running my mouth again." She slaps her hand in front of her mouth. "I should just stay quiet like they tell me."

"No, you don't have to do that," I reply, stepping closer. "I like it when we talk. Can we talk more?" I ask, lowering my head. "Please?"

Her lips part, and she seems stunned for a moment, but then she recaptures herself in the midst of a thought that made her blush. "Well, I, uh, I don't know. I'd have to—"

"It can stay between us. Just the two of us," I say, smiling.

She points up at the cameras. "They are always watching, miss."

I take in a breath and raise my brows. "I know. But isn't there like a corner where we can talk?"

She frowns. "I … I don't—"

I grab her hand tightly. She tries to pull back, but I refuse to let go.

"Please. I really need a friend right now."

The look on her face grows deeper, more emotional. And I swear, for almost a second, her eyes teared up.

Her lips part. She looks back and forth between me and the cameras. Then she sucks in a breath. "I'll call Eli."

Before I can ask her why, she's already walked out and

closed the door behind her.

I sigh. I wish I knew what it all meant. Why she'd ever want to work here.

How much money does he pay all those guards and all the staff to keep us locked here? How much money is worth the price of chaining someone's soul?

Within minutes, the door opens again, but it's not Mary who steps inside. It's Eli.

"Mary told me you needed someone to talk to." He clears his throat. "I'm listening."

I clamp the bedpost and stare at him for a moment. "If you want me to be compliant, you have to give me something in return."

A smile forms on his lips, and then he laughs. "Give me one good reason."

"Because I'll never stop," I retort, looking him directly in the eyes. "I will never stop trying to escape this place, and I think you know that."

His nostrils flare as his stance grows rigid. "What do you want?"

I swallow. "I want to see the other girls."

His eyes close, and he scoffs. "There's no way—"

"They'll behave," I interject. His face scrunches up in anger over my interruption, so I add, "I promise. We all will. I just want to talk with them."

"To discuss plans," he replies.

"No …" I take a step toward him, clutching my own fingers, desperate for a way into his heart. "Just to share our

emotions. To talk about what we've experienced. To feel …
something." Tears well up in my eyes. "Please. I'm
crumbling here. I don't want to end up like Anna."

He blinks slowly, his jaw tightening as he taps his foot.

"I only wish to get to know the others. Maybe I'll learn
something from them. Who knows, we might be able to
help each other see … our sins?" I say.

His brow rises, and that same familiar smirk spreads on
his face. "Well-played …"

"This isn't a game," I retort. "At least, not to me."

"You're right," he says, taking in a deep breath as he
paces. "It isn't. And I won't allow any of it to become one."

I stay put as he continues to barge through the room,
rubbing his forehead as though he's thinking about it. I hope
so.

Suddenly, he stops, his gaze falling onto me.

"Fifteen minutes. That's it," he says.

A breath of hope enters my lungs as I tread forward to
get closer. "Thank you."

"I wasn't finished yet," he barks, and I quickly take a
step back again. "The room will be shut off completely. No
exiting until I allow you to."

I nod. I can agree to those terms.

"You know you will be locked inside with four other
girls, right?" he says.

"I'm not afraid," I say.

"You won't be alone."

"I know."

"No, I don't think you do." He takes a step in my direction. And another one. And the next, slowly but surely coming ever closer until he's right in front of me. I swallow as he tips up my chin while towering over me. "Soren will watch over you. And if you do anything he doesn't like …"

His finger slides up my chin, across my lip, and dips into my mouth, only to drag my own saliva across my chin again. His eyes bore into mine until my lips begin to quiver, and my skin feels cold to the touch.

"Well, I think you can imagine what he'll do."

TWENTY-SIX

Amelia

When the doors to the common room open, I suck in a breath, my dress feeling uncomfortably tight even though I chose the least constrictive one. Four girls stand and sit scattered throughout the room—one on the lounge chair, one near the windows, one checking out the books on the shelf, and one pacing around the couch. But none of them is Anna.

I swallow hard as the doors behind me close. I glance over my shoulder, straight into the dirty dark eyes of Soren, his face still as unmoving as ever.

He glares at me without saying a word, and I return the favor.

Then I turn to face the ladies.

"Hey …" one of them, who wears her blond hair up in a bun, says.

I take in a deep breath and reply, "Hi."

They all look at me like I'm supposed to know what's going to happen, as though I'm going to tell *them* what to do. But I have as few ideas as they have, maybe even less. Who knows how long they've each been here. What they've been through. If they deserved what they got.

I swallow as my stomach almost turns inside out.

Why did I want to do this again? Is there even any point with Soren watching my every move? I know I agreed to him being here, but maybe this wasn't a good idea after all.

Still, I'm here, so I might as well give it a try, even if I don't know these women, and they're all looking at me like I'm the messiah for organizing this get-together.

The girls all walk away from where they were positioned and flock around me.

"Hey," the girl with the bun says. "My name is April."

"Amelia," I say.

"I'm Jane," another one with a long brown ponytail, big brown eyes, and a big smile says.

"Olivia," another girl says as she tucks her long blond hair behind her ears and blinks her bright blue eyes.

"Nice to meet you all, finally," I say, sighing. Then I look at the girl still standing by the windows. She has only glanced at me once, then looked away again, as though she's waiting for something … or someone.

"Who's that?" I ask.

April turns to look at her. "We don't know. She won't say her name."

"She hasn't said a word since we all came here," Olivia says.

"Strange, if you ask me," Jane adds, shrugging.

"Maybe she's just scared," April says, looking away. "I know I was when I first ended up in one of their houses."

"One?" I frown. "There are more?"

Her eyes widen. "You don't know?"

I quickly glance at Soren, who is still watching our every move.

April leans in and tries to whisper, "I came from—"

"No whispering." Soren's gruff voice overwhelms the entire room, causing everyone to look at him. In particular, April, whose eyes bore into his as much as his bore into hers. She swallows hard as he refuses to take his eyes off her.

"We're allowed to talk," I say.

"No whispering," he repeats.

I roll my eyes and take the girls to the couch where we sit down, crossing our legs underneath these lavish dresses in defiance of our captors.

"I came from a cult," April says, this time out loud. "One that forced women to marry men whenever they were chosen."

"Why?" Jane asks.

April looks down at the floor. "To please the men who ruled it. They called that place the Holy Ground and the people who live there '*The Family*.'"

"How strange," Jane adds.

"Tell me about it. I was taken from my regular old life straight into a cult," she says. "And then to imagine girls were born into it, thinking it was normal." She shakes her head in disbelief while staring at the floor. "You wouldn't believe what I've seen."

I grab her hand and squeeze tight. "That must've been rough."

Tears well up in her eyes as she looks up, gazing straight into Soren's eyes. Silence overcomes her, filling the room with nothing but unsaid words. "But I refused to bow to their rules. And then they sent me here to punish me or something."

Soren never takes his eyes off her, and I'm starting to wonder if he's just glaring at her like he's a mechanical robot keeping watch or if he's taking some of her words to heart. Maybe both. Wish I knew what he was doing in this house because there must be something else he's good at besides watching people. Or more specifically … girls.

"But anyway, we're all here now. How did you all get here?" April says, clearing her throat as she looks away from Soren.

"Ah … prefer not to tell," Jane says, looking away with a blush on her face.

"I'm not," Olivia says, raising a brow. "My father sent me here after I gave away all his money."

April's eyes widen while Jane's jaw drops, but me? I'm

just grinning like crazy.

"Wow," Jane says, almost choking on her words. "I did not expect that."

"I'm proud of it," Olivia says, leaning back against the couch. "He gave me a choice. Jail, death, or be sent here. So you know what I chose."

"*Chose*?" I raise a brow.

"Yeah …" Jane presses her lips tightly. "Same."

I frown. "So you all … actually chose to be here?"

They both sigh and roll their eyes as if it's the most normal answer in the world.

"But what about you, Amelia? What did you do?" Jane asks.

I gulp and make a face, clutching my hands close to my knees as sweat drops roll down my back. I look up at Soren whose eyes are still on April, but the occasional look thrown my way does not go unnoticed. I have to be careful of what I say or else.

"I … don't know. I was taken."

"But you chose this, right?" Olivia mutters. "I mean, we all did."

"Not me," April chimes in.

Unsure of how to answer, I reply, "But I don't know what I did."

They all look at me, and it makes me even more confused, more uneasy about myself. So I get up from the couch and pat down my dress.

"Do we deserve this?" I mutter to myself. "Maybe. Or

261

maybe we're all just sinners in this room. Even him." I point at Soren. "What makes him better than us?"

He narrows his fiery eyes at me almost as a warning sign not to go too far. But I've already long crossed that line.

I march over to the girl standing near the window, grab her shoulder, and force her to turn around. "You're not here because you wanna be. That's why you don't talk, right? You never asked for any of this, just like me."

Her lip quivers while her eyes fill with tears.

"Why do you let them do this to you?" I ask. "Look at how afraid you are."

"Enough, Amelia," Olivia says.

"No," I growl back.

"She was already damaged when she came here. She never talked. Don't you see?" she replies. "She can't handle your questions. So leave her alone."

"So what, you all agree with how they treat you?" I scoff.

Jane's brows rise. "I don't … think I'm being treated that badly, to be honest. I mean, we get lavish rooms, lots of food, plenty of attention."

"Because that's what's important in life," I retort, rolling my eyes.

"Maybe not to you, but to us, it's a blessing when compared to jail or something worse," Olivia says.

We look each other in the eyes. "And I think this has gone on far too long," I say, trying to stand tall even though these girls make me question my own resolve.

"We don't get to decide that," Olivia says.

"No, I think I agree with Amelia," April says through gritted teeth. When I look back at her, she's stood too.

"See?" I say, trying to inspire something in the other girls, but neither of them seems impressed. In fact, they're both just sitting there, looking at me like they wanna beg me not to start anything. And it fucking hurts.

I march over to Soren, huffing and puffing, but he just stands there near the door, arms crossed, glaring at me like I'm an ant he can squash at any moment. I'm not afraid of him. I've seen death, looked it straight in the eyes and spat in its face.

"I've seen enough," I growl at him.

His nostrils flare. He looks away, and I follow his gaze right toward April. The moment she notices his penetrative stare, she gulps again and immediately sits down on the couch, clutching the armrest like she hopes it'll protect her.

"Let me out," I growl. "Do you hear me?"

All he does is raise an eyebrow at me, and it's infuriating.

"I want to speak with Eli," I say through gritted teeth.

"Amelia, c'mon … let's talk about this," Olivia says.

"No," I reply, without even looking at her. "I want to know where Anna is. Now."

"Anna?" Jane mutters.

"The other girl," I say, and in the spur of the moment, I clutch the door handle and jerk it until the door opens just a tiny bit, enough for me to stick my fingers through.

Soren suddenly grabs my wrist, lifting my arm in the air

while grunting at me.

"Let me go," I growl at him.

He narrows his eyes at me and then fishes in his pocket and presses something, I don't know what, but a beep goes off.

Within seconds, guards burst into the door.

"Party's over," one of them says, and he grabs me and pulls me out.

"Fine," I retort. I don't even fight as they drag me away from the room. The women continue to glare at me up until the door is shut again. While they stay inside, I am hauled up the stairs. While they get to continue their conversations, I get to go back to my room.

And I'm not even sure if I mind.

***

The next day, Mary comes to my room. She doesn't say much. "C'mon."

She turns around and walks toward the door, so I follow suit.

"Where are we going?" I ask.

She doesn't answer. She simply walks down the hallway.

"Is there something important I need to see?" I ask, prodding her again. I don't care what she says.

We go downstairs, and she pauses near the dining room. The guards pull the doors open. Eli sits at the dining table. Alone. My feet are frozen to the floor.

Why did Mary bring me here?
What is going on?

Mary nudges me forward, pulling me from my thoughts. "Go on. Don't make him wait."

I swallow as I approach the table. All the seats are empty except for the one Eli is sitting in. Who would have so many seats at a table without inviting the guests to fill them? What's the point?

I sit down on my usual seat, far away from him.

Eli merely stares at me, his palms on the table as he cocks his head. One rough growl leaves his mouth. "Closer."

I suck in a breath and contemplate my options, but when I glance over my shoulder and spot all the guards standing in line, I know there are none. So I scoot my chair back and get up, shoving it aside as I walk beside the table, gliding my hand across every chair until his eyes rest upon one of them, the one nearest to him.

When I sit down, he says, "Good girl."

"Why did you bring me here?" I ask.

"I'm just curious what you thought about that get-together you had," he says, cocking his head.

I make a face. "Fine."

"Really?" He snorts. "Doesn't look like it went fine to me." He adjusts his tie. "In fact, I think you didn't like the answers you heard."

I place my hands on the table in front of me, but it doesn't stop the tension from building.

"Those girls are here because of what they did, and they all know," he says.

"They're lying," I say through gritted teeth. "You've brainwashed them."

"That's what you're telling yourself to feel better about your own decision. But you know just as well that you too chose to come here." He takes a deep breath and sighs. "You couldn't stop yourself from trying to create another uprising, could you?"

When I don't respond, he smiles at me and snaps his fingers. Out of nowhere, the servers come in with trays of food. And it's at that moment that I realize ...

Mary normally always brings food to my room around this time of day.

My eyes briskly flash from the clock to him. "What are you doing?"

"Having breakfast," he replies.

Plates are pushed in front of me while my hands begin to shake violently.

Breakfast.

That same breakfast we already shared this week.

My lips quiver. "But it's not my turn."

His eyes narrow. "Not your turn?"

He eyes me while my hand hovers over the fork and knife near my plate. For a second there, I contemplate actually picking them up and throwing them at him.

Because all of this ... feels like I just ran straight into a trap.

"Why do you think you're here?" he says.

"I only eat with you at this table once a week," I mutter, staring blankly at him.

Whose turn is it? And why aren't they here?

"And now you eat with me twice a week," he replies, grabbing a piece of bread. "Rules change."

"No, they don't," I retort. "Not with you."

Right before he shoves the bread into his mouth, he pauses. "What do you really want to ask me? Spill it."

I hold my breath, my heart pounding so hard it feels as though it's about to explode from my chest. There is only one thing that changed. One person who could possibly cause him to suddenly deviate from his regular schedule.

Anna.

"Where is Anna? What did you do with her?" I ask, grinding my teeth as my body begins to shudder. "Why isn't she here?"

He takes a big bite from his bread and swallows it down before answering. "You don't have to worry about her."

My eyes widen.

She didn't talk to me for days, and I thought it was because of something I said. But maybe she's been gone all this time.

Nausea overtakes me, and I scoot back my chair as far away from the food as possible.

What if they punished her for trying to escape with me?
For trying to kill herself?

Eli gazes at me as though he's waiting for my response,

but there isn't any.

None of this is right.

This is all a test.

My pupils dilate as the realization of this simple truth hits me. It's as if all the blood leaves my face.

What if they hurt her?

What if she's dead?

My hand covers my mouth to stop the squeal from spilling out.

It's my fault. I made her run.

And as I get up, Eli doesn't take his eyes off me. Not even as I stumble away from the table toward the door. Not even when his guards block my way, their arms folded, stance menacing.

Eli raises two fingers into the air and snaps them.

"Let her go," he says, his voice guttural ... almost like that of an animal. "I'll catch her soon enough."

TWENTY-SEVEN

ELI

When she gets up and flees the room, I let her go.

She'll be allowed to dwell on her thoughts. But not for long.

I intend to follow suit, the beast inside me getting hungrier by the second. I admit, I enjoy the hunt more than I should, but it's a weakness of mine. So I take one more bite, pat down my mouth with a napkin, and get up to pursue her. My guards immediately step aside for me. They know not to meddle in my affairs, even if I break the rules. I can change them how I see fit.

As I leave the dining room, Amelia has already rushed to the top of the stairs. She pauses near the banister to take a peek over her shoulder. When our eyes lock, it's as if the world ceases to exist, and all that's left is her and me.

"You can run, Amelia …" I say as I slowly go up the

269

stairs while she storms toward her room. "But I will always win."

With a devious smile on my face, I fish the key to her room from my pocket and swirl it around my finger until I get to her door. When I open it, she's in the corner, busy with something behind a curtain.

As I close the door behind me, she jolts up in shock and backs away against whatever she was doing there. I wonder what else she hasn't told me. Because I sure do wonder how she ever managed to escape and take Anna with her.

She grows rigid as I approach, her body tense while she leans against the table. But her eyes are skittish, searching for something, anything. I warn her with a deadly look, and our eyes connect in fury. The flames can almost be felt from across the room.

In a split second, she rushes at me and tries to slap me, but I quickly grasp her wrist just before her palm hits my skin. I'm far stronger than she is, and I've easily bent her to my will, forcing her hands down. We're right up in each other's faces, the look in her eyes so vivid and clear that it excites me. Because she has rarely ever looked at me like that before.

Like … she actually thought of killing me for the first time.

Magnificent.

"You can't win this fight, Amelia," I say as she struggles. "Give up."

She pouts, tears welling up in her beautifully enraged

eyes, the look so pretty that I could just swipe her off her feet and fuck her right here, right now.

"What did you do to her?" she asks.

"She's not well, so she's being taken care of."

She scoffs. "That's a lie. She's dead, isn't she?"

I wonder how she came to that conclusion. Is it because of the breakfast I wanted to share with her? I'm surprised she managed to figure out that Tobias, Soren, and I have it with each of our guests. I suppose it was only a matter of time, especially with her talking to the others. Still, I'm amazed at her wit.

I smile, tilting my head down. "Is that what you fear the most? Death of your friends? Or the death of you?"

She resists me again, trying to free herself even though she knows it's no use. She's never been this combative, and I'd be lying if I said it didn't make me as hard as a rock.

"Stop fighting. Anna is safe. And once she's healed, she will be free," I say, my brows to show I'm serious.

"Free?" she growls, throwing me a look.

"When she allowed Tobias to take control, to punish her for what she did, she freed herself from the burden of shame," I answer.

Amelia breathes in and out slowly. "And I'm supposed to believe you?"

"Yes. It's the truth."

She rolls her eyes in a way that makes me want to bend her over my lap and spank her. "That's easy for you to say. You make the rules."

"And I also abide by them. Which is why I'm setting her free when she's healed," I reply. My grip on her wrist grows tighter as I pull her closer to me. "Now tell me exactly how you two escaped."

"Or what?" she retorts. "You're going to force me to stay in this room until I die of old age?" Her chest rises and falls faster and faster as her eyes search mine for a hint of mercy. I've certainly hit a chord.

A pearly bead of sweat rolls into the crevice of her tits. My eyes can't help but traipse down as my tongue dips out to lick my top lip. Her body quivers as her eyes pull away from mine to look back at that spot she was standing at mere seconds ago when she was fumbling with the curtains.

My eyes narrow, and I step aside quickly to tear them away. Behind it is a vent leading to the other room. So this is how they forged their little plans.

I grab her shoulders and shove her against the wall. "You were talking with her."

She makes a face. "I did what I had to do to survive."

"Survive?" I repeat, grasping a strand of her hair to twist it around my finger. "Is that what you think this is?"

"You're punishing me for something I can't even remember," she hisses through her teeth.

"You asked for this. Yet you refuse to behave like the others," I reply.

"Because you make it impossible!" she spits back. "I've been kept in this room like some pet, and you think it's strange I'd want to talk to someone?"

I cock my head. "You wanna talk? Talk. I'm listening."

She slams her lips shut. "As if it's that easy."

"It is," I retort. "If only you would let yourself open up to me …" I tip up her chin, forcing her to look at me instead of trying to look away. "Anna did to Tobias."

Her pupils dilate. "I don't believe it. This is all just more mind games, isn't it?" Tears well up in her eyes. "You had her killed, didn't you?"

I laugh, and it makes her face contort even more.

"I know you've killed people. I just know it," she says.

I lean in, my grip on her body growing firmer and firmer. "How can you tell?"

Her eyes flick back and forth between mine. "I …"

A fully-fledged smile forms on my lips. "Or is it just that you see"—I tap her forehead—"what you want to see?"

She swallows, visibly shaken by her own confusion and betrayal of mind. She's unraveling before me, and I want to swallow every delicious speck of her destruction.

Oh … she's really outdone herself now.

***

Amelia

I stare into those fiery eyes filled with ruin and pain. Behind those eyes, a monster hides in plain sight. But something else is there too, something beyond that anger and domination … something I can't quite decipher, but I know it's the key to unlocking all of this madness.

A part of me wishes I could undo what I just did. That I could stop myself from trying to hide that vent. That I hadn't ever spoken to Anna in the first place so she'd be safe. So she wouldn't try to run into the water all by herself just to end things.

But I can't change the past, and now Eli is here, and we're facing off again. And for the first time, I feel like I've finally taken a bit of power back from him.

I managed to deceive him. Not for long, but long enough to bolster some defiance and show that I'm resourceful. Cunning, even. And the smile on his face proves that I surprised even a man like him.

"You've been lonely, haven't you?" he asks. "Longing for my presence like a solemn little angel."

The urge to slap him again grows too strong. My hand rises, and he doesn't intercept this time.

SLAP!

The sound is harsh. Brutal. It even surprises me.

A red mark appears on his skin as my hand lowers, my lips parting in shock at what I just did.

I swallow hard, staring at him, wondering what he's going to do. If he's going to punish me. Yell at me. Hurt me.

Instead, he leans in and smashes his lips against mine.

My eyes widen, and I just stand there, accepting this kiss as though I'd been waiting for it all this time. His mouth on mine feels almost natural, as though it was always meant to be there, and it shakes me to my core.

I should fight him, punch him again. Instead, I only want to kiss him back. But it's wrong, so wrong, so I bite him.

He inches back, touching his lip. Blood seeps from a single cut as he hisses, "You bit me."

My eyes narrow. Suddenly, he grabs the hand I hit him with and pins it behind me as he spins me on my heels and pushes me face-first against the wall.

"You surprise me, time and time again ..." he says. "Fighting me every step of the way, yet you still said those words: Punish me."

"What about Anna? Did she ask for any of this?" I reply, glancing at him over my shoulder.

"Anna was sent to us. You weren't."

"You *took* me," I spit back.

"And you said *yes*," he retorts. "And from that kiss we just shared, I'd say that was what you truly wanted."

"I thought ... I thought ..." I mutter.

I don't even know why I said it or why I even let him

kiss me, and I can't ever take it back.

"Is this what you want?" His grip on my wrists tightens, and he pushes himself up against me, body to body. "For me to ravage you as Tobias did to Anna just to make her confess?"

"Do it then. Take me. Use me," I growl back.

I'm tired of fighting … fighting not just him but my own desires too. And if giving up my body means I finally get to learn why he took me, then I'll take that chance.

His teeth grind, and his nostrils flare. He leans in, his head resting on my shoulder, his breath against my ear sending goose bumps down my entire body. "Beg."

"What?" I gasp right as he places a soft but merciless kiss below my ear.

And for some reason, my head inexplicably tilts as if it wants to allow him access to give me more.

"Help me help you," he whispers.

I can't believe I'm actually thinking about it, but I am. So I ask, "How?"

His lips quirk up into a smile against my skin. "I will fuck your memories out of you."

I gulp from his raunchy words and the mere thought of him plunging into me. I hate this man for trapping me here, but I hate him more for actually making me want it. For actually making me want to … beg.

"Please," I murmur, my voice soft, almost angelic like. "Do it. Fuck me."

He groans, the sound making my pussy wet already.

Why? I don't understand. My body responds to every touch, every kiss like it desires it more than anything. From the minute he laid his eyes on me, I wanted nothing more than for him to kiss me. But if I'd known it would cost me my freedom, would I have ever even said a word?

Every time we talk, I want nothing more than to throw daggers at his heart, but when he's close, I only want him to take me.

What's wrong with me?

Why do I desire that which I shouldn't ever crave?

"As you wish," he whispers into my ear.

Suddenly, his hands are on my breasts, and he rips apart the top of the dress like it comes easy to him. In one go, he tears it down until my breasts pop out, and he grabs them with both hands. My jaw drops in shock as he plays with my nipples, tugging at them and twisting them in ways that I never imagined possible. But most surprising of all is my body's reaction … and how badly I want him to continue.

I've never felt anything like this before. No one has ever touched me like this, not even Chris.

It's like Eli's been overtaken by some mad desire to claim me—own me, even—and it brings chills to my bone.

And every kiss he plants on my skin makes me want it more and more even though my mind is telling me not to give in, not to say yes to this man, this beast.

But how could I ever win this fight if I'm not the one playing the game?

I'm merely the pawn, and he's the master player, toying

with my soul.

"Is this what you had in mind?" he whispers, tearing down the dress even farther to make a point. "Or this?"

His hand suddenly moves away from my breasts, sliding underneath my dress right where my ass is. There are no panties, no one gave me any, and they're not in my wardrobe either. And when he touches my ass, I almost jolt up and down against the wall.

"So much you have yet to learn ..." he says.

"I'm not some innocent virgin," I spit back. Why am I trying to convince him? I don't understand why I even care. But when he talks to me, I can't help but fire back. As if I have this need to prove myself ... to prove him wrong.

He smirks. "Oh, I know."

When his finger slides across my pussy, I lose it. A whimper leaves my mouth almost instantly. Am I truly that easy? Or am I just ... hungry for so much more?

"But you sure seem to be enjoying yourself," he muses as he flicks my clit. "Are you?"

"Don't flatter yourself. You're not my first," I retort.

"No ... but I will be your last," he growls.

I have no time to respond as a finger plunges inside me. My mouth forms an o-shape, and I have to bite my tongue to stop the moan from spilling out.

"You think you know how this goes. That a man takes what he wants and leaves it at that," he says, circling my clit again. "That's what you're used to. What you were given by the countless men who came into your life and used you to their heart's content."

He plunges in again, thrusting not one but two fingers inside so deep that I can barely stay upright.

"But none of them ever gave you what you truly needed, did they?" he mutters, biting his lip when he sees me squirm. "None of them made you beg."

He folds his hand up to cover my pussy as he slams inside time and time again, all while playing with my nipples until they're taut. My eyes almost roll into the back of my head from sheer pleasure. Right then, he pulls out and continues circling my clit, playing with it until I'm on the brink. My heart beats in my throat, my lungs rapidly expanding as I try to keep up with the breaths that are slowly turning into moans.

"Please," I whisper, breaking apart at the seams.

"Please?" he repeats. "Please … what?"

"Do what you want with me," I murmur, drowning in lust.

Suddenly, he flips me around against the wall and shoves me against it, fishing something shiny from his pocket. Not one thing … but two.

Clamps.

My pupils dilate, but the only response I can give is a yelp as he attaches both of them, one to each nipple.

There's a chain attached to the end, and he tugs at it, groaning with glee at the sight of my pain.

"It hurts," I squeak.

He licks his lips with delight. "Punishments aren't

supposed to be fun, angel."

His free hand dives back between my legs, circling my clit until I'm so hot and bothered that I can't see straight anymore. The whole room feels like it's swirling as he plunges his fingers inside my pussy, his other hand nudging the clamps secured on my nipples, wreaking havoc on my body.

"Fuck …" The word slips from my mouth with ease. I'm so close to falling apart that I can barely stand.

Our breaths intermingle against the wall in this tiny corner of the room. "Yes, come for me," he murmurs. "Give your all to me."

And as he flicks his index and middle finger across my pussy, my body explodes into delicious spasms. I buckle against the wall while he holds me upright with his body alone, his erection poking my thighs, promising more.

And I'd be lying if I said all of it didn't turn me on.

In fact, my pussy is as wet as can be. Rarely have I ever had such a powerful release. Not even when he strapped me to the bed and turned on those vibrating panties. No, this was on another level entirely, and it makes me despise myself.

I fell apart right in his arms, and it was exactly what he wanted.

I handed it to him on a platter … my own defeat.

TWENTY-EIGHT

ELI

"Please."

The moment she uttered that word, she lost.

Not just the game ... but also her dignity. Her pride. Her wrath. All of it lost to me with a single word.

And I can't help but savor the taste of her fall.

I told her I was going to be here, waiting for her to take the plunge.

And now she finally begged.

I'm not going to let this moment go to waste.

I grab her body tight, pushing her closer to me as I relish this moment of pure sexual debauchery with my finger still inside her wet, aching pussy.

Since the day I met her, I've wanted nothing more than to claim what she had to offer. But it had to be her choice, her request, her wish that brought her to me. That made her succumb to me. Because now she's in my hands, left at my mercy with no other options than to obey.

Obey and maybe she will finally find the truth behind her own demise.

In this world, there is no decision without consequence, and she must pay the price. She wants to be free of guilt, free of suffering? She must earn her way out.

And now that she's finally ready to surrender ...

I'm ready to take what belongs to me and fuck her into oblivion.

***

Amelia

Panting, I look up into his eyes, and it feels as though my soul is slowly returning to my body after being ripped out. "Fuck me then," I growl, enraged at myself for giving in so easily ... and for enjoying it too. "That's what you want, isn't it?"

He pulls his fingers out of me, and I try not to react even though I feel like I lost something I wished to keep. And he brings them to his nose and takes a whiff. The groan that follows awakens all my senses.

He brings his fingers to his mouth, and his tongue dips

out to take a lick. "Delicious …"

Chris never said that. About food, yes. About me? He wouldn't dare. But Eli says it as though I'm the best thing he's ever tasted, almost like a compliment. And it makes the goose bumps scatter on my skin.

Suddenly, he spins me around again to face the wall, and he pushes my dress up, throwing it over my back to expose my naked ass. He rips down his zipper, pulls out his cock, and grips my waist tight. Before I can say a word, he's plunged inside deep.

With a gaping mouth, I yell, "Fuck!"

My breasts bump against the wall, nipples still sore from the clamps squeezing them together. It's as though he can read my mind because one hand immediately moves to my tits and tugs at the chains once again, releasing delicious spasms of pain throughout my body.

He groans as he thrusts inside harder and harder, almost as if he wants to shove me straight into the wall and break it. "Say it then. Say the words, and I might give it to you."

His cock feels so big inside me that it feels as though he'll never fit, but he does. And the mere size of him has me delirious already.

"Please …" I whimper as he throws every inch of his weight into pounding me.

I'm not thinking straight. I can't. Every one of his thrusts sends me to the next level.

"What am I?" he growls.

"You're my punisher," I say.

He smacks my ass so hard I squeal. Wrong answer.

"What am I?" he repeats, his voice more strained than before.

"You're my owner," I reply, hoping that's what he wants to hear.

But he spanks me again, this time on the other cheek, and the sizzling pain makes his thrusts all the more pleasurable. It feels so damn wrong. I shouldn't like it, and I hate that I do.

"What. Am. I?" he growls.

Another spanking, thrice on each cheek. My ass must be gleaming red by now. My skin burns with pain. Is this the punishment he meant? Or is there much, much more?

"I'm here to save you," he says. "Now let me fuck the sin out of you."

He grabs my hair, twisting it into a bun with his fist as he plows inside endlessly. The longer he goes on, the more I'm losing my grip on reality. All I can feel is his length buried inside me while my face is squished against the wall, my hungry pussy begging for more.

How could I have fallen so fast, so deeply?

How could I love this as much as I do?

Logic fails me as he wraps his arms around me, greedily grasping my breast with one hand while the other clutches my waist. He continues to pound me harder and harder until our breaths and sweat mingle, and the line between right and wrong is blurred. If this is punishment, then I don't even know if I wanna be good anymore. It's sinful and divine all at the same time, and my mind is spinning as he turns my head and smashes his lips on mine.

The kiss is heady, needy, as though he's been holding back all this time, and it ends just as roughly, as though he has to tear himself away with a roar.

Right then, he buries himself inside, and his warm seed fills me to the brim. I gasp as he presses another delectable kiss against my neck, his teeth sinking gently into my flesh as he falls apart. Even though it's mere seconds, it feels like time is standing still as his arms are still wrapped around me in an almost sweet embrace.

I could almost, almost forget about the fact he robbed me of my freedom.

We're both panting when he pulls out of me, and I hate that it leaves me feeling barren. He gazes at me, the look in his eyes changing from pure lust to unfettered indignation, which makes my lips part in confusion.

He spins me on my heels and takes off the nipple clamps, tucking them back into his pocket without even looking at me while I try not to hiss from the burning pain. He zips up again and adjusts his clothing while his back is turned to me. I pat down my dress as I fight the flush spreading to my cheeks. After all this sexual frustration finally boiled over in both of us, I didn't expect him to finish like ... that. It's almost as if he regrets it.

But that doesn't make sense. This is what he wanted ... right?

He wanted to punish me with whatever means

necessary, including sex.

Unless this was supposed to get me to talk.

"This isn't going to work," he says.

"What do you mean?" I ask.

He straightens his cuffs, his back still turned to me. "You enjoyed that, didn't you?"

Now I truly can't stop the red-hot flash from spreading across my cheeks. "I … I …"

"You don't have to say it. I know the truth," he adds.

I look away, embarrassed by my own desires.

"Don't," he says, glancing at me over his shoulder. "Do not feel pity for yourself."

"I don't," I say, tucking my hair behind my ear. "But you did all of this to punish me, didn't you?"

He turns away again and sighs out loud.

"And it didn't work," I add.

He suddenly marches for the door, so I say, "Wait!"

His hand still lingers over the doorknob.

Even though I hate what he's done to me, how he's made me yield to lust, I can't fathom being alone again in this claustrophobic room. "Please … don't leave me alone in here. I'm begging you."

He opens the door again but falters halfway, his fingers digging into the wood of the doorjamb. "I cannot give you what you need."

"I won't ask you to free me," I say.

"Then what do you want?" he says, licking his lips as he throws me a look.

I swallow. "Please, let me see Anna."

He frowns. "You care so much about a woman you barely know?"

I nod.

His brows furrow, and he looks away for a split second. "Tonight."

And then he waltzes out and closes the door behind him, leaving me to the merciless onslaught of my own devilish desires for a man I shouldn't ever have let in.

TWENTY-NINE

ELI

I blow out a few breaths and pace the hallway for a moment, contemplating whether I should put my fist into the wall, but I know that won't do me any good. But so much emotion is swirling through me right now that I can barely control it, and it's eating me alive.

Never was keeping a girl from escaping so difficult.

But more importantly … neither was making her submit and confess.

I guess that's what you get for picking her yourself, for wanting more than you can bargain for. But I needed to have her. I chose her so I made myself a promise that I'd watch her until she'd sin, and then I'd swoop in to take her.

If only I'd known that not just my own lust would get in the way but that my own heart would be at stake too. That this obsession of mine would turn into something more than a carnal need for justice. I crave to punish her more than any other, and it's making me feel things that I never thought I'd feel.

When I took over this House, I vowed to keep enforcing the rules and follow them no matter the cost, but my own desires have gotten in the way of that. And now I actually gave in to them.

I slam the walls with my flat hands, the pain a small reminder that everyone sins, even me.

I have sinned so badly that I can't even think straight.

The only thing coursing through my mind right now is the unbearable need for more of those delicious lips as I kiss my way through the night while I bury my cock deep inside her. I want to hear her moan, listen to her beg, see her unravel in front of me.

Not just for punishment. Not just to make her confess.

I want to do it because I *can*.

Because I want to take her, use her, fuck her, *own* her.

I want it all, and I could take it all as it's within a fingertip's reach.

But … that's not why I brought her here. It's not right. Men like us aren't supposed to crave or enjoy the lust of life. Men like us aren't supposed to live.

We were made to punish the weak and make them confess. To fight for justice as we were taught.

But the more time I spend with her, the more I'm beginning to realize that's just not enough for me.

I lean my head against the wall and close my eyes for a

second, trying to center myself.

Clearly, harshly fucking her didn't work. It didn't bring out any of her pain, didn't make her remember, which means only one option is left.

Going deeper ... and darker ... until there is no way back.

Because she must face her demons, and I must face mine.

After taking a few more breaths, I march right into the recovery room downstairs. Only two beds are taken this time, one by the guard Amelia injured and the other by Anna.

And next to her bed is Tobias, sitting in a chair while he holds her hand.

When he looks up at me, the unbridled anger I see in his eyes would ward off any man. Except me, of course. I know better than to fear a fellow brother in this House.

"How is she?" I ask, closing the door behind me.

"The same," he replies, his grip on her hand tightening as he focuses on her eyes. "What are you doing here?"

I sigh. "Looks to me like I'm not the only one who has stepped over the rules."

He throws me another enraged look. "I don't need you to check up on me."

"I'm not," I say, holding up my hands. "I'm just saying ..."

"Keep your comments to yourself," Tobias replies, focusing on Anna again. "You're the reason this even happened in the first place."

I grab a chair and sit down opposite of him, watching as he caresses her cheeks.

"She didn't deserve that pain," he says.

"She took her punishment into her own hands," I say.

"Your girl did," he barks back. "It's her fault Anna is in this shape."

"She escaped," I reply. "I took every precaution."

"It was not enough!" he spits, his hands shaking as the tip of his finger touches her lip. "You should've never brought her here."

My nostrils flare as I try to stay calm. "I already told you why I did it. But I think you understand now." I look at Anna and how she's lying there so at peace even though her mind must be in turmoil right now. She looks like an angel washed up ashore, desperate to cleanse herself of her sins. I can see why he fell for her.

"Don't," Tobias growls. "We're both in the wrong here."

"And neither of us intends to stop," I reply.

He's quiet for a second while gazing woefully at Anna.

The beeping of the machines goes on and on, silencing the storm raging in my heart.

Could I have done something to stop Amelia from escaping and taking Anna with her? If I had told her what Anna had done, how she was feeling about her own sins, would it have made a difference?

None of it matters. Nothing can change the past. What's

done is done. Anna is here now, and all we can do is wait until she gets better.

"Tell me why you're here," Tobias asks. "And don't give me lies."

I laugh a little. "I wouldn't dare." I lick my lips. "In fact, I indulged myself in one too many."

"Oh, yeah?" He raises a brow. "You? Lying to yourself?"

I shrug and look away. It takes me a while to speak. "I ... kissed her again."

When I finally gather the courage to look at him, he's staring right back at me for God only knows how long. "It's only going to get worse, isn't it?"

I roll my eyes and snort. "It's the only way to get through to her."

"You tell yourself that," he says.

"And you keep telling yourself that you don't do the same thing," I spit back. I clear my throat to ease the tension in the room. "She's close. I can feel it. I just need to push her a little further."

"And?" He raises a brow. "You wanna ask me something?"

"She wants to see Anna."

He scoots his chair back and immediately gets up to point at me. "No. No way am I allowing that girl close. It's because of her Anna almost died!"

"Anna almost killed herself," I say. "Amelia didn't know she was going to do that. Even though they have been talking."

He makes a face. "How?"

"Through a vent in the room." I wave it off like it's no big deal. "I'll get it fixed."

He runs his fingers through his hair. "I can't believe this."

"It explains why Amelia chose to take Anna along with her," I say.

"How did they even do it?" he asks.

"I don't know. She won't say, but I'll find out sooner or later," I reply. "But if we want these antics to stop, we need to ensure she confesses. And for that, I need her to confront her own guilt."

"You mean, confront Anna," he says.

"It might help her," I say.

Tobias sighs out loud and sits back down again to grab her hand and softly caress it.

"I promise you, she will be safe," I add.

He looks up at me. "I want to be there."

"Deal," I reply. "As long as she gets to have her moment."

"I don't want any of that escaping nonsense happening again. Not under my watch," he says. "Anna was already done here. Her confession was completed. And Amelia ruined everything."

"I know, and nothing about that has changed. Once she's healed enough—"

"I don't want to talk about it," he interjects, his voice

stern. "Just go. Do whatever you want. Leave me."

I nod. When he doesn't say another word, I turn around and walk off. As I open the door, he suddenly speaks up again. "They'll be our end. Won't they?"

I pause, contemplating my answer, but I realize there is none. None that would fix this impossible problem we've created. "She'll be here tonight."

***

Amelia

Nothing compares to seeing someone you care about lying motionless in a hospital bed. Wires and tubes come from Anna's body, her pale face in stark contrast to the beautiful shine I saw mere hours ago when we both ran for our lives.

My heart is going a hundred miles an hour in my chest. At least, that's what it feels like when I look at her as she lies there lifelessly and still like a doll wrapped in a thin sheet. Tobias sits beside her, guarding her with a watchful gaze as I enter the room.

I dare not make a sound, afraid he might jump me if I do.

But Eli said I could see her. Mary personally came to get

me and escorted me here, so Tobias must have known I was coming. But I still don't feel welcome.

I swallow as the door softly closes behind me, and I step closer from the shadows. The beeping of the machines feels like a reminder to breathe, each breath heavier than the one before as I get closer to the girl who's supposed to be Anna.

What happened to her?

I sit down on the empty chair opposite Tobias and stare at her, wondering if she has any life in her left. If she got what she wanted after all.

"How is she?" I ask.

"Not well," Tobias replies with a stoic voice, but the underlying hurt doesn't escape me. He looks up at me, tears forming in his eyes, but he blinks them away quickly. "Severe pneumonia."

I frown and look down at her, unable to stop myself from grabbing her hand. But she's icy cold. "Will she make it?"

"I don't know." He slams his lips shut and looks at her with so much love and adoration that I freeze up. I've never seen a man look at a woman like that, not unless … they were in love.

But that can't be right. She's his captive, and he's the bad guy. She couldn't have liked him, right?

But what if she did, and I'm the one who convinced her not to?

A painful pang hits me right in the gut as I curl up and make myself tiny. Guilt is like a parasite, eating you up from the inside out, and it's gotten in my stomach.

I look away before it gets to be too much.

Maybe I was wrong. Maybe she didn't want to leave. Maybe … she just wanted to be understood.

He squeezes her hand so gently that I feel like I'm intruding on a personal moment. Warmth oozes from his body as he leans over and slides a few strands of hair from her forehead.

How could these men be so cruel yet so kind at the same time?

I don't understand any of this, and it's driving me insane because I'm starting to question who is actually the bad guy here. Is it them … or is it me?

Anna's in this bed because of me. She escaped thanks to me, and then she sought to end it all. If I'd known, I would've never taken her along. But I didn't ask. I was too focused on my own problems that I couldn't see clearly. I was selfish.

"I'm sorry," I say, swallowing back the tears when he looks up into my eyes with the most solemn look I've ever seen.

"Okay," he replies.

"Okay?" I repeat.

"What do you want?" he asks.

"I … I …" I mutter. "I don't know."

"Sorry doesn't fix this," he says.

"I know," I reply, shaking my head. "But I just wanted her to know I didn't do it on purpose. I just—"

"You just wanted to escape. And you brought her with you ... so she could die," he says.

"No," I say, licking my lips as a tear rolls down my cheeks. "I didn't know this was going to happen."

"But it did," he barks.

He's not giving me an ounce of forgiveness. Not even one single iota. And it hurts.

I lower my head between my shoulders. "If I could trade places with her, I would."

"No, you wouldn't," he says. "And I don't want you to." He caresses her again. "She deserves better than that."

I nod a few times, sinking away into the silence. "She did ..."

He glances up at me with a serious look on his face. "She *will* get better."

I hope he's right. I pray she does. Because if not, her death will shatter my already brittle soul.

"You might think what we do here is wrong. That it's heinous. Criminal," he says. "But some people need this. Some people ... heal from this."

Maybe he's right. Maybe some people really do need this. I just could not understand because I didn't know what it was like living with the guilt. But now I do.

If Anna really did get her parents murdered ... she must've been living with so much guilt.

Even if she wouldn't admit it to herself, no one can do something so terrible without snapping their own heart in two.

I wonder if she would have gone through with it if she knew what it really meant.

If she knew how much hurt it would cause, even to herself.

Maybe she realized, in the end, it wasn't worth it. That her boyfriend convinced her to do something she really didn't want to do. And then she stopped wanting to live.

I sigh to myself.

Poor Anna. If I could take away the pain, I would.

"If I had known what she … did … I wouldn't have taken her with me," I say.

"Because having your parents killed is terrible and inhumane?"

Well, that's bold. I didn't want to say it like that, but I guess he's right.

I suck in a breath. "Because she needed to face what she did. And I stopped her from doing that."

He gazes at me for a moment, the look in his eyes sincerely surprised. Then he nods. "What we do here is necessary."

"I understand now," I reply.

"Do you?" he reiterates, lowering his head.

"I …" I don't know what he wants me to say.

That I was wrong?

That I just didn't know that we truly deserved all of this?

"So you believe us now when we say you are here for a reason?" he asks.

I take in another deep breath and look at Anna for a

second. She knew. She knew deep inside her heart, yet I managed to convince her otherwise.

"I just wish I knew why," I say. "Anna knew."

"If you're truly ready, you will know what to do," he says.

My lips part, but I don't know what to say.

Tobias looks down at Anna again and cocks his head tenderly. "She was ready."

"I'm sorry," I say. But no matter how many times I say it, nothing will make it okay. Nothing will make her okay again. Except time.

But I will not sit idly by and let myself befall the same fate.

Even if I deserve everything I've got coming for me.

THIRTY

ELI

The moment my door creaks open, I already have a smile plastered onto my face.

She's here.

I knew she would come. I've known since the minute I left her in her room to think about her actions while I brooded here in the dark.

I didn't just let her visit Anna out of kindness. There was a chance it would finally lead her to the right conclusion, so I took the opportunity, and it paid off.

She isn't as innocent as she once believed.

And now she's here to come and find out why.

I'm quietly reading my book in the middle of my study on my comfy armchair near the fireplace when she enters. The door closes softly behind her as she comes closer and stops on the red carpet right in front of me.

I lower my book to meet her gaze with a penetrative stare.

"I'm ready," she says.

My tongue darts out to wet my lips. Right on schedule.

"Are you sure?" I raise a brow.

She nods, standing tall and proud even though I think she knows damn well what she's asking from me.

"I deserve the truth," she says, swallowing hard. "Show me what I did."

My eyes narrow as adrenaline rushes through my veins, filling me with excitement. I put aside the book and lean over on my elbows, tapping my fingers together. "You deserve …"

"Punishment."

My cock became hard just from that word spilling out of her mouth.

A grin tugs at my lips as I lean back in my seat and watch her. "Beg."

She sucks in a breath and licks her lips. "Please … punish me for my sins."

I could listen to her say those words every second of the day.

Instead, I jump up and charge at her, clasping her throat in a single hand. She shudders, beads of sweat rolling down her forehead as I tilt her head backward and look at the pale skin underneath my fingers. She's vulnerable, completely at my mercy … perfect.

And all it took was a nudge, a single instance of seeing

the truth in front of her own eyes.

All this time, I was searching when the answer to the problem was right in front of me.

She saw in Anna what she could never see when she looked at me: Her own guilt.

And now she's come to repent.

Her crystal clear eyes peer straight into mine, and I can't help but feel moved. She came to me out of her own free will. And now I will be her undoing.

I push her down, down, down until her legs cave underneath her, and she slowly kneels on the carpet. I go back to my armchair to sit down again and continue watching her, wishing I could see into her mind.

"What do you think will happen now?" I ask, rubbing my chin.

"You will do whatever you want with me," she replies with a sigh. "And I will obey."

"Why?" I ask. "Give me one good reason."

We stare each other down for a second. Her answer is the single most important thing right now, and there is only one right one.

"I don't want to be free. Not without knowing why I was here. I need to know. I want to know the truth. To confess," she says, every word costing her more of her soul.

A wicked smile spreads across my lips. "I've waited forever for those words."

A blush spreads across her cheeks.

"And what do you think I want you to do?" I ask,

cocking my head.

She's silent for a moment before twisting her hand behind her back and peeling away the zipper that holds her dress together until it falls to the floor and leaves her completely naked on her knees.

I'd be lying if I said it didn't turn me on and make me rock hard.

As I shift in my seat, the burning pain in my back is a constant reminder of what it costs me to go over the edge. But for her, I'm willing.

"Come," I say.

She gets up as I command her to and walks over to me. Her pink, supple body is such a pretty sight to behold, especially in those high heels.

"Why did you take off your dress?" I ask.

"Isn't that what you want?"

"Perhaps," I mutter.

"I've been wondering … Why did you give me only dresses to wear?" she asks.

"Because it's what you wore that night," I reply.

Her face grows stone-cold as though she's upset she can't remember, but I can.

If only she knew.

My hand inches forward, and I touch her naked waist with a single fingertip, dragging it all the way down over her belly button until she gasps. "And unwrapping is half the fun," I reply, stopping right before her pussy.

Her cheeks flush again as her lips part. "I'm sorry, I

thought—"

I swiftly plant a finger on her lips to make her stop. "Don't think. Just feel."

My other hand slides down her thigh to her knee and back up again until her entire body is covered in goose bumps. Then I lean over the side of my seat and grab the knife sitting in a block. Her eyes immediately widen, and her body tenses up. I hold her in place as I bring the knife close.

I look up into her eyes. "Don't. Move."

It's not just a command. It's a dare. A dare to see this through until the end.

And as I drag the knife all the way from her knee up to her pussy, she shudders in place, fear striking her hard.

"What are you so afraid of?" I ask, narrowing my eyes as I slide the blade across her sweet, pink skin, wishing it was my tongue instead. I run it across her belly and go all the way to the top, circling her nipples until they're peaked. "Do you think I'll hurt you?"

Her lips quiver. "Maybe …"

"Do you think I could?" I ask.

She nods.

"Do you think I *want* to?"

Her lips part, but she hesitates.

I stop and pull it away from her, leaning back into my chair just to admire the view. "Sit," I growl, and I pat my lap.

She does what I ask, but not without the inner turmoil clearly showing on her face. But she begged me to do it …

so I will give her everything I have to offer.

Her ass feels so good against my pants that I find myself fantasizing about biting into it. Maybe another time … after.

She eyes the knife like a hawk as I slide it along her arms and down her back until that too creates goose bumps on her skin.

"What are you doing?" she asks as she glances at me over her shoulder.

"Desensitizing," I reply.

"Oh …" she murmurs. "I thought you were contemplating where to slice me."

I snort and bite my bottom lip. I'm not content with a one-time show. I want more. I want everything, and I want it *forever*.

So I slam the knife into the chair's armrest right in front of her. She jolts from the fright. I take the opportunity to grasp her wrists and pin them to her back, fishing a pair of cuffs from the drawer in the desk next to me so I can bind them together. She's at my mercy now, completely helpless on my lap, left to my every whim. And she doesn't even flinch.

"Don't hold back," she whispers.

I tilt her head back by her hair. "Oh, trust me when I say I'll be anything but gentle."

I immediately rip down my zipper, take out my cock, and lift her up and down again, right on top of my shaft. Her mouth forms an o-shape, not fast enough for the sound to come out, but fast enough to register the fact I've buried myself deep inside her aching pussy.

All this time, she was lying, telling herself she didn't want me, and now her pussy is already wet just from a single devious touch.

"You're my little angel, aren't you?" I growl, fucking her harder every time her ass ends up back on my lap. "An angel who did a bad thing, but who wants to remember so badly she'll do anything for it. An angel desperate for love."

She bounces around on my lap as I fuck her hard and fast. "Yes," she mewls.

"Say it! Tell me you're my angel!"

"I'm your little angel!" she cries, making me fall harder and faster than ever before.

And I pull her head back sideways and force a kiss onto her lips as I thrust in hard and mercilessly.

She doesn't pull back even though I expected her to bite. Instead, she deepens the kiss, her lips opening to allow me access, which I greedily take. My tongue swivels around inside her mouth, desperate for more. She tastes divine, like walking sin ready to be devoured, and I want nothing more than to claim her for myself. Not just today, but forever.

And it hurts to know that I can't keep her with me, despite wanting to more than anything. After all, those are the rules. We're supposed to set them free when they've been punished and repented. But will I be able to let go, knowing it will cost me everything?

I don't want to stop kissing her. Don't want to stop fucking her every orifice. She is mine, and she should be mine forever. Can't I have both?

I groan against her lips, and she only kisses me harder as though my moans turn her on as much as hers turn me on. When our lips unlatch, my hand dives between her legs, and I flick her clit as she bounces up and down on top of me. We're both delirious with need, lost in sin, and neither of us cares. Because this is what she needs. What *we* need. Complete and utter surrender.

Her body sways with the rhythm as I'm sure her eyes are already rolling into the back of her head. The delicate skin on her back is covered in goose bumps and salty sweat, and I lean forward to lick it off, savoring her taste.

Right then, she tilts her head back, and I press a soft but passionate kiss on the side of her neck. The moan that rolls off her tongue as she writhes on top of me pushes us both over the edge. I bite down into her shoulder until my teeth draw blood, and she yelps. Her pussy clenches around my length, milking me until I roar out loud, and we both come together. Explosive doesn't even begin to describe us. But I am falling harder and harder for Amelia. She's the only one who's managed to break the barrier of ice around my heart.

With a raspy breath, I undo the cuffs around her wrists and place them on the table.

Suddenly, she swirls around on my lap, grasps the knife, and holds it against my neck.

It happens so quickly that I don't even realize it until it's too late.

We're both still panting, my cock still hard inside her,

but that doesn't stop her from putting the knife right against my throat. The point pushes into my skin until I tilt my head back far enough into the cushion of the armchair that she and I are looking eye to eye.

And I stay there for a moment, both our bodies frozen in time even as the clock ticks away steadily. All that can be heard are our rapid breaths coming from our red-hot lips. Sweat trickles down her chest into the beautiful crevice between her tits, the place where she hides all the secrets to unlock her heart.

But I've finally managed to puncture through.

A devilish smile spreads on my face as her eyes lock with mine. "Do it," I growl. "Kill me."

The look on her face darkens, her teeth clenching as she contemplates her options. I can feel the sharp pain of the blade cutting my skin, but I ignore it. Her eyes flicker with rage, fear, and guilt all at the same time, and it's consuming her whole.

"That's what you want to do, right?" I say, and I grab her wrist and push the blade farther against me until the blade digs into my skin, drawing blood, which oozes down the blade. "Just one step away."

She shivers in place, a tear rolling down her cheek. Still, she doesn't relent. But the pain in her eyes … I've only seen that kind once before.

In the mirror.

"Look at it," I growl. "Look at the knife."

Her eyes follow my direction to the blade, and they

widen slowly.

"You did it once. You can do it again," I say.

Her lips quiver, her grip on the knife slowly disintegrating until it finally drops to the floor. "I can't."

But surprise overtakes me when instead of taking out her rage on me, she leans in and kisses me.

***

Amelia

Tears, sweat, and sex all mix in this simple but devastating kiss. I don't know why I felt the urge to kiss him, but the second I saw the blood run down the knife, I knew I had to stop. I didn't want to hurt him, even if I hate him for what he's done to me.

For what he's made me remember.

Because this knife … isn't his.

It's mine.

When our lips unlock, I can't find it in me to push back, to lean away, to get off him. My body is frozen in place as I stare at the red droplets rolling down his neck. The same blood I saw that day my whole world caved in on me.

"This is my knife …" I stammer.

"You remember it now … don't you?" Eli whispers, his

eyes still on me like a hawk.

But my mind is slipping further and further away into the unknown, into the memories I thought I had lost but were merely banished to the back of my mind.

"I did it," I mutter as Eli licks his lips and holds me steady on his lap. "I ... killed him."

"Who?" he asks, clutching my face with both hands. "Say his name."

A single tear tumbles down my cheeks as my lips part, the depravity of my own actions breaking me in two. "Chris."

THIRTY-ONE

Amelia

Birthday night

After a long day of working in the library, I couldn't go home. Not until I had emptied at least two bottles of wine. I didn't mean to get drunk, but when you're all by yourself and your birthday is celebrated by contemplating your relationship with your cheating boyfriend, that's what happens.

I'll have the biggest hangover tomorrow, but I don't care even the slightest as long as I can bury my head in the sand. When I finally get home after the bartender kicked me out, I take a deep breath before I open the door as I'm expecting Chris to be waiting for me. I'm not looking forward to it, but I know we need to talk. So I shove my keys inside and throw my bag on the dresser.

"Chris?" I call out in my drunken voice.

But there's no reply. Not even a sound.

Where is he?

I walk into the living room and come to a cold, hard stop.

There are clothes littered all around the apartment floor and furniture.

Women's clothes.

I gulp.

No. No. This can't be happening.

That kiss was a one-time thing, right?

He wouldn't bring a woman into our home—our bedroom—right?

Suddenly, the door to the bedroom bursts open. Chris stands in the doorway, half-naked. A storm brews on his face, and the moment he sees me, it's like a volcano erupted in his eyes. "You … You're not supposed to be here."

His nostrils flare, rage flooding his face.

Suddenly, he charges at me, and he shoves me all the way to the kitchen island, his hands wrapped around my throat.

It's not the first bruise, or the first cut, or the first hit. But it's the first real threat to my life.

Panic fills my veins, and I instantly go into fight or flight mode. I try to squeal, try to shove him off me, but it's no use. He's much stronger than I am, and my drunken body is unequipped to deal with the situation. I claw at his fingers, biting my own lip in the process, but nothing works, and I'm fading fast.

No time to think. No time to act.

"Chris …" His name is the last word that leaves my lips.

The last word before I grasp behind me, desperate to escape … And my hands find one of the knives from the wooden block.

And in one quick jab, I've lodged the blade right into his chest.

His hands lower as he stumbles away from me. I grasp my throat and inch away as he sinks to the floor. But something in my mind clicks. Something wicked. Something cruel.

And instead of running, instead of calling for help, I stay and watch him drown in his own blood.

***

Present

My lips feel icy cold against his as images of a cold-hearted bitch stabbing her own boyfriend to death spring into my mind. Memory after memory comes flooding back inside.

Blood seeping from Chris's wounds. Him falling to the ground like a bag of potatoes. Me not giving a single care in the world if he lived or if he died. And when I pulled that blade from his soft flesh, I smiled.

I actually smiled.

The one person who could hurt me, really hurt me, no longer could.

Because I hurt him instead.

I back away from Eli slowly as the tears spring into my eyes. "I … I …"

"Tell me what you did," Eli murmurs, grabbing ahold of my face.

"I stabbed him," I say, hiccupping. "I'm a murderer."

"You killed him because he was going to kill you," he says.

My eyes skid back and forth between him and the memories lodged deep inside. "Oh God, oh God."

"Look at me, Amelia. Look at me." Eli holds on tight, keeping me here in the moment. "Stay with me. Don't lose yourself."

"I can't. I'm a killer. I did it. I … I … I'm a monster," I mutter, unable to keep the weeping at bay. "I'm sorry. I'm so sorry."

He shushes me and pulls me into him, wrapping his arms around me so tight it feels like I'm suffocating. But it's not the same kind of chokehold that Chris had on me. It's a warm embrace, one filled with love and acceptance, one where I can let go and cry until I have no more tears left.

"You're not a monster," he says.

"I stabbed him!" I yell through my own tears.

"You had no other choice," he says. "Kill or be killed."

I close my eyes and let the full depravity of my actions wash over me like the ocean water washes over the beach.

This is what Eli meant when he told me I needed to face my own sin. The sole reason for me wishing I would be punished over and over again.

I didn't know. I couldn't remember.

But now that I can, the memory is eating me alive.

All I see is Chris and his blood-drenched chest, eyes wide open, begging me to help him. And I refused.

"Please ... make it stop," I beg, my fingers digging into Eli's shoulders as images of Chris's dead body flash into my mind.

I was drunk. Foolish. And so out of it that I must have stumbled out of my apartment and ran as hard as I could. Until I no longer had the will, no longer had the energy ... and collapsed in the park. Where my brain locked itself out of the memories it needed to hold close ... just to protect me.

There's no other explanation for me losing so much time, and I'm only now starting to remember glimpses of this frightening reality.

"I can't take them away," Eli says. " I told you, it would be harder than anything you'd ever done. This was never going to be easy."

"Why did I want this?" I mutter. "I would've been better off not knowing."

"Because your soul knew it needed to release this. Your

mind was drowning in pain," he replies. "And now you've released it from the burden of keeping it a secret."

He's right, but I don't want him to be right.

I sniff, trying to cope with the immense feelings overwhelming me. "It hurts. It hurts so much."

"I know …" he whispers, and he tilts his head down and presses a soft kiss onto my forehead. "But I will be here every step of the way."

"Why? Why didn't you call the police if you knew? Why didn't you have me arrested?" I ask.

He looks at me, and for the first time, it feels sincere. "Because this is what we do. We punish the sinners until they repent."

I lean back and lick my lips. Even though I'm completely naked, I've never felt this warm and comforted before.

As weird as it may seem, skin to skin with my chest against his is the only place I feel safe right now as though he is the only person on this earth who could understand what I'm going through.

"All this time, I thought you were lying. That you were keeping me here for your own dirty needs," I say as I listen to his heartbeat, the sound keeping me in the here and now. "But you were just trying to make me see the truth."

He lets out a long-drawn-out breath. "And now you know why."

"How did you know what to do?" I ask, frowning.

His brows rise. "It isn't sex. It's what the brain does

when it is in pleasure mode." He taps his temple. "You shut off and allow yourself to leave all your presumptions, your self-consciousness, and your insecurities behind. And it allows me to apply certain … tricks to get you to see your own sin."

I swallow hard. "The knife."

He nods.

That same knife I used on Chris is now on the floor right beside this armchair. I almost tried to use it again, but I couldn't.

Not just because the memories flooded back inside … but because deep down, I couldn't hurt the man who had brought them back.

The man who feels as though he was sent to judge me.

The man who I thought was my punisher.

But is he really?

Or is he my savior?

His thick chest muscles tense as he wraps his arms around me and gets up from the chair.

Enough? What is?

"What are you doing?" I ask, wishing we could just stay there for a moment so I could bask in his warmth and forget all my sins, if only for a moment.

"Shh," he whispers.

The air he exudes is both powerful and peaceful at the same time. Like a man wishing to save me, and I can't help but feel at awe at his commitment. At how he did all this to me just to show me what I had done. Just to make me remember.

And for some reason, I feel grateful. "Thank you."

The words slip from my mouth before I even realize it, and he stops and looks down at me for a moment to smile. It's the most genuine smile I've seen on his face since I first met him, and it warms my heart.

"Don't. Please, don't," he says, clearing his throat. "I don't deserve that."

"But you helped me remember," I say, frowning.

His nostrils flare. "I did what I had to do to save you. That doesn't make me a good guy."

"I didn't say you were." My hand reaches to touch his face in a moment of pure need for love, even if it's the wrong kind, but the look of suffering he gives makes me stop.

"Don't," he says. "Please, don't. Don't thank me."

My hand inches back, and I swallow. "Sorry."

"It's not that I don't appreciate it," he says, and he continues walking. "It's that I don't deserve it."

He takes me to a door on the other side of the study, which leads straight into a bedroom. His room. The room I was never welcome in or invited into, one that was locked when I still had my privileges to roam about the house.

The oversized bed in the middle of the room is large enough to fit five people. The curtains in front of the window are already closed, but I can still check out the room because of the small light next to the bed. A black leather couch sits in the back next to a giant wardrobe and a mirror that spans the wall from top to bottom.

But I don't have more time to look as Eli places me down on his bed, fierce protectiveness in his eyes as he lies down beside me and pulls the blanket over us.

He wraps his arm around me and pulls me in closer until we're spooning. Like we're an actual couple.

But that doesn't make any sense. He doesn't love me. We're not together. He's my captor, and I let him do this to me because I asked for it. Because I pleaded with him to punish me, and now I got my wish.

"Don't think too much. You need to rest now," he says, tucking me in tighter.

The warmth in his arms almost makes me forget who he is. Almost.

"I can't. I can't sleep after all this," I say, trying to force myself to remain in the here and now and remember he is the bad guy, even when the lines are blurring.

"Then at least rest," he replies with a stern voice.

"But I need to know more," I say as I clutch the blankets that smell like him a little closer, afraid of what'll happen if I admit that maybe, just maybe, I feel something for him. Not love … but adoration. And I know that isn't right. I'm not supposed to feel these things for a man like him. My captor.

Especially when he knows so much about me. Things I didn't even know myself.

Because Eli never told me why he knew what I'd done to Chris. Or how he got that knife.

I swallow hard. "I have questions."

"What do you want to know?" he murmurs against my skin, the warmth of his breath almost distracting me enough not to want to ask.

I'm tired, so tired. Not just from fucking but from reliving the trauma I've tried so hard to keep buried.

My eyes can barely stay open, yet I know I must hold on. No matter how hard they wish to close, no matter how hard my brain wishes to forget. I must know the truth that's right in front of me.

All I need to do is ask.

"How … did you get that knife?"

The question hangs in the air for so long that it feels suspended in time. His body no longer feels warm against mine but cold to the bone, and I shiver in place.

"I found it in your home," he says.

The words reverberate over and over in my mind.

In my home.

He was in my apartment.

He was *there* when it happened, that night.

My eyes are wide open. I'm awake. I'm fully aware.

Memories flood back into my mind of the day I found myself lost in the woods and stumbled back home, when I looked out the window and saw a man leave. He was leaving *my* apartment. Eli.

But why did he come to my apartment when we'd only met a couple of times before? Even if he knew where I lived, he couldn't have possibly known what was going to happen … that I was going to kill my own boyfriend…

Unless…

He did.

###

THANK YOU
FOR READING!

Thank you so much for reading Dark Wish. Make sure to pick up book two, Dark Lies as well! Now available on Amazon.

You can also stay up to date of new books via my website: www.clarissawild.com

I'd love to talk to you! You can find me on Facebook: www.facebook.com/ClarissaWildAuthor, make sure to click LIKE.

You can also join the Fan Club: www.facebook.com/groups/FanClubClarissaWild and talk with other readers!

Enjoyed this book? You could really help out by leaving a review on Amazon and Goodreads. Thank you!

ALSO BY
CLARISSA WILD

Dark Romance

The Debt Duet

His Duet

Savage Men Series

Delirious Series

Indecent Games Series

The Company Series

FATHER

New Adult Romance

Cruel Boy & Rowdy Boy

Ruin

Fierce Series

Blissful Series

Erotic Romance

Hotel O

Unprofessional Bad Boys Series

The Billionaire's Bet Series

Enflamed Series

Visit Clarissa Wild's website for current titles.

www.clarissawild.com

ABOUT THE AUTHOR

Clarissa Wild is a New York Times & USA Today Bestselling author with ASD (Asperger's Syndrome), who was born and raised in the Netherlands. She loves to write Dark Romance and Contemporary Romance novels featuring dangerous men and feisty women. Her other loves include her hilarious husband, her cutie pie son, her two crazy but cute dogs, and her ninja cat that sometimes thinks he's a dog too. In her free time, she enjoys watching all sorts of movies, playing video games, and cooking up some delicious meals.

Want to be informed of new releases and special offers? Sign up for Clarissa Wild's newsletter on her website www.clarissawild.com.

Visit Clarissa Wild on Amazon for current titles.

Printed in Great Britain
by Amazon

84226332R10187